WOVEN WORDS PUBLISHERS *Presents*

THE BALLOON GIRL

By

Syeda F. R

Syeda F. R. belongs to the City of Pearls, Hyderabad. She has done her MBA and has a degree in education. She had been a member of the Quality Assurance Team for a year in an MNC in Hyderabad. Prior to that, she had taught in a school in the Middle East. As she loved being with children, she got back to her passion - teaching. At present she works as an English teacher in one of the reputed schools in Hyderabad. She is also an editor at Woven Words Publishers.

An avid reader herself, she has been penning down words and lines since she was a student. She writes for her blog and for online poetry groups/sites.

Her first work, Love & Pain in Verses, was a collection of poems with which she stepped into the writing world. She writes short stories and poems. She is working on her first novel and hopes to bring it out next year.

You can reach out to her on Twitter: @SyedaFR

Instagram: @sfr.world

Facebook: https://www.facebook.com/SyedaFRwrites/

The Balloon Girl

Syeda F. R.

Woven Words Publishers OPC Pvt. Ltd.
Registered Office:
Vill: Raipur, P.O: Raipur Paschimbar, Dist: Purba Midnapore,
Pin: 721401, West Bengal, India.
www.wovenwordspublishers.net
Email: editor@wovenwordspublishers.net

First published by Woven Words Publishers OPC Pvt. Ltd., 2017

ISBN-13: 978-81-934093-8-1
ISBN-10: 8193409388

SHORT STORIES

Price: $12

Printed and bound in India

Acknowledgements

The journey of my life has been enriched by the presence of very beautiful people. I am making a futile attempt to include most of them and I fear that I may forget someone. The fact remains that each person whom I have met in this life has left an impression, a mark on me. So I take this opportunity to thank each one of you for being there in my life.

My family has always been like the life support system for me. Every time I felt dejected or depressed, they provided me the love and care I needed. My siblings and my children have always given me the courage to move ahead and do what I wanted to do. And it is my better half who deserves accolades for the patience and troubles he has had to endure while I sat hitting the keys of the keyboard. Yet, he always pushed me to complete what I had started.

I want to thank my lovely colleagues and friends who have always encouraged me to finish this book. Their words of praise and advices have always made me learn and strive further. Thanks Josh, Saniya Chawla, Preeti De Sarkar, Qizra Fatima, Meraj Fatima, Imran bhai, Anmol and Sanjana for your trust in me. Tahmeena di, thanks for making me feel that I have the ability to do this and for waiting for this one.

My talented friends Sarah Abou El Ella, Jennifer Greene, and C.M Blackwood, made me realize that we can achieve our dreams. My first set of readers included Sanaa and Saloua Kerroumi, Somi, Yogeshwary, Anu and Priyanka who have always been too kind to me.

I would also like to thank Mosiur Rehman, who hasn't just been a publisher for me but a friend, critic and guide as I began this journey into the world of written words. I'd like to thank the team of Woven Words Publishers for turning my dreams into reality.

I extend my gratitude to the ones who have been my teachers and also to those who call me their teacher. I shall always try to make the former proud of me while I try to make the latter the best for the society. I would also like to thank two author friends of mine who inspired me very closely, Marilyn Grey and Fia Essen.

No word of thanks can be enough for the Creator who has bestowed His blessings so abundantly upon me that I fall short of words. It is His blessings that I have the little knowledge to use words. It is His mercy upon me that I am able to make my dreams come true. It is indeed His gift to me.

I wish to thank **you** too. I thank you for trusting in me and reading this book of mine. It is the support and love of you, the readers, that will encourage me and many other writers like me to keep writing. It is your love and support that will drive us to work more, write more and tell more stories.

Thank you for the love you have for me.

Keep smiling.

Spread happiness around.

Stay blessed.

Love,

Syeda F. R.

To the people I shall remain indebted all my life,

Mummy and Daddy!

Index

Adam meets Her

Walking down the lane, she looked around. The darkness around the young woman engulfed everything but the radiance emanating made her stand out. She stepped ahead while the coloured balloons attached to long delicate threads - tied to her hand - swayed around. With an innocent smile on her face, she walked ahead. She knew exactly where she had to go. Distressed people need a helping hand. People of those kinds pulled her towards them. Always! She knew where and when she was needed and she had to be there at the precise moment - to make it a special one.

There is no crime committed by man, as deplorable as making a woman wait. Being a man, I had committed this crime. Now only a miracle could save me. I prayed for it all along the way to the altar, galloping my way to the guillotine.

R u coming Adam?

I checked her last message again. The question had come nearly an hour ago. After the meeting I had messaged back asking if she was still there, though I knew it was in vain. My message might have reached her fifteen minutes ago and she hadn't replied.

I rushed towards the restaurant, where I had promised to be at eight for dinner. It was close to my office, so I didn't bother to get my car. Traffic could delay me further, I knew.

It was ten now. I knew she was going to be mad at me. I was late for dinner, not by minutes but by hours. Two hours to be precise. While she had reached there on time, as usual.

Why did these meetings come up at the last minute!

Why did it have to come up when I had decided to propose to her?

Tonight was going to be the special night. If the board of directors hadn't called in for the meeting, I would have slipped the solitaire ring across her fingers by now. Not today though. I was caught up in the urgent meeting called by Susanna. How I despised her for tonight's crisis!

That's when the phone beeped. With hope building in my heart, I checked it and when the name flashed, I heaved a sigh of relief.

WAITING!

The message seemed scarier and I walked the rest of the distance in a dilemma. I groped through the pockets of my coat and felt the bulge of the box. I knew the square cut solitaire was just perfect for her style and fingers. A smile crossed my face thinking how beautiful it would look on her finger.

I reached the restaurant and saw her sitting at the table I had reserved for us. Dressed to kill, she sat like a calm ocean, deep in thought as she kept clicking the keys on her laptop. She was working on her new project, her dream of becoming an author. The only saving grace here was that she had used the time in writing a few pages and I hoped that she wasn't as angry as I had perceived her to be.

She sat undeterred with serenity around her. It was like the calm before the storm wreaked havoc. As I walked closer, she raised her long fingers and flicked the few strands of hair that were falling on her face. She tucked them behind her ear with soft graceful movements. Those fingers created music whatever they moved on. She had worn a brown pencil skirt with a cream colored top. The elegant top left her shoulders bare. She was my love. My Maria!

We had met a year ago. Since then we were steadily moving ahead in our relationship. Every day was a day of falling in love more deeply, like a quagmire, sucking us within. I wanted to get bound to her, forever.

Contrary to her outward appearance of peace and serenity, her face showed anger and tiredness. She had been waiting here for me after a tiring day at office. She had stopped taking my calls after an hour had passed. I was sure that she would stay there, because, that's how she is. If she left, then there was no way I could gain her mercy for at least a fortnight or a month.

Hope and intuition made me come here and I thanked my stars for that. Now the only question was - how was I going to propose to her when she was so furious? Furious at me.

Just then her eyes met mine. Her glittering green eyes glowed with fury. The corners of her eyes had smudges of kohl. Tears usually did that to them. My heart ached for it was something she didn't deserve. I had spoiled the most awaited moment of my life; the one that should have been the most memorable for her – for us.

I slowly walked towards her. Her eyelashes fluttered as she tried to avoid seeing me come closer. I took the seat before her and heaved a sigh. Was it of relief? Bad guess!

As soon as I had taken my seat across her, I swiftly opened the button of my blue coat and pulled my tie loose. Feeling the corners of the ring box in my pocket, I sat upright. I had to assure my heart that I would give it to her soon. If only Lady Luck would be kind to me here on.

Everything made my breathing difficult - the exhaustion of work, the sudden unplanned meeting, the suppressed anxiety of my heart and the silent wrath of the woman I loved.

As if God sent, the waiter approached our table.

"May I have the order now, Ma'am?" he asked her, stressing on the word 'now'. I flinched as I knew what danger loomed upon me.

Her eyes warmed up to him.

"Oh yes Jim. I'm sure my guest would like to have something. For me, just get a plain lettuce salad with olive oil. Diet Coke with that please."

A smile spread across his face. I wish he could infect her with that smile. At least then she would smile at me for she was reciprocating to his smile so calmly. Filled with jealousy, I cleared my throat. He looked at me and gave the same polite smile. Damn these hotel staff! Why do they smile so much? Somehow his smile seemed to tell me that he knew I was the 'to-be-slaughtered' lamb. There was an 'I-know-it-all' glint in his eyes.

"What shall I get for you, Sir?" he asked with the same polite manner.

"Get me the same then," I replied blankly, keeping down the menu card which I had picked up.

The entire universe seemed to have plotted against me in these two hours. I was too nervous to think of hunger, but at the most unacceptable time, my empty stomach decided to let me down, for it started rumbling. It growled as though a starving elephant breathed within it. I hoped no one had heard. The smile across the waiter's face blew away that hope. The smile showed that the message had been broadcast in public.

"Get him mashed potatoes and a steak. A little spiced and smoked than regular, and a Diet Coke for him too," she ordered.

A smile broke on my lips and the heartstrings played a symphony of happiness.

The waiter nodded his head as if he were a slave writing down the orders of the queen on a parched roll.

"That was just what I wanted," I said with a smile as soon as the waiter walked away.

"I know," she replied as coldly as the ice in the freezing boxes of the mortuary.

God! Women!

They can be the warmest of all people at one moment and turn into the coldest in the next. Just like that - with a snap of the fingers.

I stretched my arms across the table and held her hand in mine. It was warm. She was usually like that. Warm and soft hands with long slender fingers. The soft, flawless, fair skin was smooth and the nails painted in browns and maroons complemented it.

Tonight they were decorated with a dark brown shade, like her skirt. I turned her hands palm side up and passed my fingers through hers. Her fingers didn't wrap themselves around mine. Clear signal - I AM MAD AT YOU!

I felt helpless and started tracing letters on the pale skin of her palm.

A slow and sultry curve to make an 'S'.

A soft and simple ring to make an 'O'.

She tried to pull her hand away, but I firmed my grip on it. She didn't try anymore.

Moving my fingers gradually twice to make 'R's.

Then the letter 'Y'.

I looked into her eyes and saw the same aloofness in them. I knew she had every right to be furious at me. I had not done anything intentionally. With hopes of undoing the mistake, I raised her hand, and let my lips touch the soft palm. I planted a kiss on it.

My eyes looked at her face through the gaps of her own fingers, and there was a slight curve on her lips... A smile on her face meant - a tiny ray of hope. A small victory!

Slowly she pulled away her hand as the waiter was standing near us and had started transferring the plates of food from his tray to our table. The aroma of the steak filled my nostrils and I felt like a dam break open in my mouth. As soon as he turned to walk away, I hastily began devouring it.

She slowly ate her salad. I couldn't convince her to order more. I was already a convict, so I wasn't in a position to insist or convince her to listen to me. It was more than enough that she was at least smiling at me, with her anger leaving her like waves washing away from the shore. We kept sipping on the Coke, slowly even after the food was over.

As my hands moved into my pockets, my eyes were locked with hers. They always kept me captivated, as though in a spell. My fingers reached the wallet, when I saw her eyes widen in surprise.

There was a strange rising of eyebrows and the dilation of her pupils.

What was that for?

The waiter walked in with the check. I took out the credit card and handed it to him. He left as silently as he had come. Suddenly the vibes between us had changed. Raising my eyebrows, I tried to ask her. She lifted her fingers and traced across her neck, signaling me to check mine. As my eyes shifted towards the collar of my white shirt, I was shocked.

There were marks on my collar. Not some random marks, which could be forgiven. Even blood marks or the vampire's teeth marks wouldn't have given me the shiver which these marks caused.

Those were marks of red. Deep red stains. Crimson marks of lips. Lipstick to be exact. Then it struck me.

Just after the meeting, while the board members were leaving, Susanna had hugged me. We were working on the team together and the black suits were happy with the progress we had made.

Our reports were progressive and we had just won their confidence to take the project ahead.

Now I need to tell a little about the lady in question. Susanna was our CFO - Chief Financial Officer. She was a smart woman, beautiful too. She was a professional businesswoman yet witty and fun-loving personality. The problem was that Maria believed she had eyes on me. The fact was that *Maria hated her.*

The embrace had been just a casual one when she thanked me and told me to enjoy the weekend. How would I convince the curious tigress who sat judging my case? I hadn't even begun to defend my stand, when the waiter returned with my credit card. She quickly rose from her seat and before I realized she walked past me. Collecting her coat, she slipped out of the glass doors while I followed her.

'Oh dear Lord! Not this. Not now,' I thought to myself.

I ran behind her, but she wouldn't stop. I called out her name. Unperturbed she kept walking faster; I reached up to her and held her hand. We had stopped at the corner of the square, on the pavement. There was a lamp post and a wooden bench a few steps away. I knew I could explain it all to her, if only she would sit and talk.

I pulled her back. When she turned her face, it was enticing to see her eyes shine under the light of the street lamp. My heart skipped a beat and seemed to forget to take the next.

Though it may sound annoying or foolishness, but I loved it when Maria got jealous. She wasn't someone to feel insecure, but being jealous is something women just can't hide or avoid. It showed how much she loved me. It meant she wanted me for herself. Just what I wanted to do – to make her mine forever.

"What is it, Mr. Adam?" she asked sarcastically trying to wriggle her hand out of mine.

"I am sorry Maria. I didn't mean to keep you waiting and these lipstick stains, I can explain," I pleaded.

"I know you had a meeting. I know those are Susanna's. Let's wind up for the night now Adam," she said angrily.

Anger seething through her, she firmly spoke, "I just want to go away for now."

"No! Not yet. I want to tell you something very important. Listen to me Maria. Please," I said. All was in vain. She had wriggled her hand away from my grip, and briskly walked away to her car. The only words she said were, "Good night Adam."

I knew she meant it. Helplessly I saw her drive away. I always hated to leave her alone when she was angry. I wanted to hold her and tell the whole thing to her. Plead forgiveness. Pacify her. Convince her. I was already aware that she wouldn't listen. As with all men, I never knew how to go about it. Should I really leave her alone or go after her?

Wondering what I should do next, I filled my lungs with a deep breath. I took a few steps back and sat alone on the bench.

I had done it; I had messed it up. I sat there rubbing my eyes. Excitedly I had called her in the evening and planned the dinner. How ridiculously the evening had ended! I closed my eyes and Maria's face stared back at me.

"Hey!" A sweet voice reached my ears.

I opened my eyes and turned my head, with a tiny hope of seeing Maria. As I had expected, it wasn't her. It was a young and innocent face with a beautiful smile. She was lovely, glowing like moonlight in the darkness of the alley. A young woman, probably out for a party after college. It was the weekend after all.

"Hi!" I replied uninterestingly.

"Can I join you here?" she asked in the same soothing voice.

"Yeah. Sure. Anyway, I am leaving now," I replied with a heavy heart. I started to rise from the bench.

"No. Wait. Don't go," she said. Something made me do as she said. I sat back on the bench.

For the next few moments she didn't speak, neither did I. The wind blew coolly around us and the balloons in her hand swayed, doing a ballet with it.

Suddenly she asked, "Why do you look so sad?"

"Nothing. Just a tiff with my girlfriend," I remarked sadly.

"Whom.... you were going to.... propose to?" She teased while she pulled the threads of the balloons.

"Yes," I replied lost in my own thoughts, as I turned my face towards the full moon shining in the sky.

Suddenly it struck me, how did she know?

"How do you know?" I enquired turning my face to her.

She gave again that innocent smile and said, "Look at you. You look so sad as if she had already rejected you."

I smiled. She smiled back.

I took a deep breath and pressed my hands on the bench to raise myself up. I was just going to rise, when she spoke softly, uttering one word at a time.

"Don't...worry... so…much."

I looked at her and wanted to thank her for the concern.

She continued, "She won't say 'No'. She is waiting to hear it and may even return any time now."

I looked at her dazed. Maria was a strong-headed woman. She would not listen to me for the whole night now - maybe for a couple of days from now.

"You don't know her," I remarked, "She won't talk to me for days now."

"Why don't you buy these balloons? Then let's see what happens." She pulled out a red, heart shaped balloon and thrust it towards me.

Aahhh! A smart seller. How cleverly she was making me buy her balloons!

"Oh c'mon! It doesn't happen that way," I smirked.

"Let's just try it," she said and handed over two red balloons to me.

Impressed by her business tactics, I held the balloons in my left hand and pushed the right hand into my pocket. I pulled out my wallet to pay her. Suddenly a car screeched and stopped in front of me. Instinctively, I raised my head. My heart jumped about as the glass of the window rolled down and to my great surprise there was Maria.

"What do you plan to do here Adam?" she asked me in a concerned tone.

"I don't know. I was just...," I fumbled with words in my mouth.

"Anyway, what are you doing with those balloons?" she asked stepping out of the car. She folded her hands across her chest and stood leaning on the car, waiting for my answer.

"These? I bought them from this girl....," I looked around, but there was no one. Where had she gone? She hadn't taken the money for the balloons.

"Aww! They are so beautiful Adam," Maria exclaimed with joy. Banging the door of her car, she rushed towards me and took them from my hand.

"You don't know how romantic you look holding them for me," she said, planting a kiss me on my cheek.

I pulled her into an embrace as I kissed her forehead. I always loved to do that. I knew she loved it equally. How much I had wanted to do this since I saw her at the restaurant! We stayed like that for a few moments. In sheer silence, under the moon's silver light we stood drenched with the soft moonlight.

"You wanted to tell something important to me?" she asked me while we stood on the pavement, raising her head. Her hands were placed in mine. I recalled the balloon girl's words, 'SHE IS WAITING TO HEAR IT.'

I stopped thinking further. I looked at her beautiful face. Her complexion was glowing in the darkness. All her features enchanted me - her thin lips and perfect nose, the doe eyes and her long eye lashes. She looked at me as though waiting for something more. I stood close to her, and held her hands. I wanted to see her face closely while I spoke those words. I began before anything went wrong again, without losing out any more time.

"Maria, will you be mine forever? I want to live each day, each moment of my life with you. I want to see you when I doze off, and when I rub off the sleep from my eyes. I want to hold you in my arms when we celebrate my success, and fall in your arms when I need comfort or support. I want to be known as my love's husband. I want you to share my name with me. Will you make my wish come true?"

I put my hand into my pocket and took out the box which was waiting to be opened. With the other hand, I pulled the upper part of it away, revealing the stone under the light of the street lamp and the moon. It sparkled like the stars embedded in the sky. I watched her closely. The moment was precious. I saw her eyes as they grew larger with surprise, her lips opened wide. Her hand flew to her mouth. A tear spilled out of her eye and rolled down her cheek.

"Oh Adam! I thought you would never say this. I have been waiting for this for so long," teary-eyed Maria said as she jumped into my arms.

"Yes, my love! I want to become yours forever," she continued as she wrapped her arms around my neck.

I held her close to my heart and whispered 'I love you' in her ear. With a soft murmur she said the same. Tonight it felt special. It felt like the whole world was vanishing away. Only the moon was the silent witness to our vows.

Just then I saw her. She was walking across the road, with her little red balloons. She turned and glanced at me with that infectious smile.

I silently mouthed the words 'Thank You' to her. She blew a kiss towards me, towards us. She turned back again and walked away with those little balloons of hers flying in the air behind her. She was special, but the question in my mind now was....

Who was this balloon girl?

Matthew's Princess

The city was all lit up. Ahead she walked into the alley. She smiled as she walked alone, humming a song of love on her lips. Her bright red, pink, yellow, green and blue balloons kept swaying and bouncing along with her. She kept trudging along and knew where her steps would take her; to the place where she was needed. She kept walking. She was.... the balloon girl.

Sarah was angry, she was furious. She had waited for hours for him but he still hadn't turned up.

Just when she wanted him, he was not there for her. This did not happen always, but very often. Every time when she needed him around, he wasn't there. He always missed her special days, her school events and a few of their special plans too. A couple of promises of dinners outside were broken, a few donuts of chocolate were forgotten, and a few movies were missed.

It had been fine while she was too young to mind it, but not now. Earlier she would forget it with the blink of the eye. As soon as he'd return with a little surprise, she'd forgive all. Today, it was beyond her ability to forgive and maybe even to forget.

She couldn't bear this. He'd missed the day. He had forgotten the promise. He had broken her heart. He had shattered her dream of a perfect day.

How could he afford to miss it! Unbelievably he had missed her 12th birthday. She was extremely angry at the only man in her life, her father.

Matthew knew that he was going to have a tough time ahead. He hadn't been able to say NO to his senior manager when he had asked to stay for a few hours extra after his usual timings. There was a sale in the department store and the crowd was becoming uncontrollable for the rest of the staff. He had recently joined the store as the floor manager and couldn't afford to lose the job. On the other hand, he desperately had wanted to be there for Sarah.

His little daughter whose 12th birthday he was missing.

He kept calling up at home and spoke to her. He heard her sad voice and unspoken feelings. The burden of guilt became heavier as minutes passed by. He had to ask her to cut the cake, and let her friends enjoy the party. His words of comfort were useless for her. He knew how much she wanted him to be there. He knew how much he had longed to spend the day with her.

After the crowd had receded, he had been able to trickle out of the store. Leaving instructions, he had pulled his jacket and walked out of the doors. He wore it as he walked, while the cold wind seemed to hit like a whip on his back. His breath formed little clouds of smoke, as he hastened towards the bus. He again called up to know about Sarah.

Sophie, his wife told him that Sarah was quiet and sad, in her room. He was in grief too. He just hoped that the little gift he had brought for her would make her happy, and she would forgive him for his mistake.

The party had ended and her Dad hadn't been with her, he hadn't kept his words. He had broken her little innocent heart - his lovely daughter's pure and loving heart.

"Dad, you know what?" she would ask often, and continue, "You are the best Dad in the world!"

Her words echoed in his ears and pained his heart. She always told him that. He had proved her wrong. How cruel destiny was! Sitting in the bus, he flicked through the pictures in the gallery of his mobile phone. He stopped at the picture he had taken when her eyes had sparkled when she saw the cake. It was saved in his phone for always. She had loved the cake.

He had brought it home after finishing the decorations of the living room and the hallway. It was a big, white vanilla cake with her favourite character Rapunzel smiling across. The confectioner had done it wonderfully.

He was Matthew's friend and knew the cake was for his little princess. He had done a remarkable job with it. He stared at the smile of his precious daughter, which was the last thing he had seen before leaving home. The grin plastered on her face as she was running around analyzing the streamers and decorations and preparing her accessories to match with her little red dress.

They had promised to get her the red dress when she saw it one day while returning from dinner. It was expensive, so they had to save for it by squeezing through the household expenses. The smile of her lips, and the glow on her face was worth every little thing they had let go to buy that dress.

That's the love that runs as blood in the body of parents.

With a lot of difficulty, Sophie had convinced her to cut the cake and have fun with her friends. As a mother she was always caring and loving, and as a wife she was the best support a man could have. Sarah loved her so much that she'd hide her sadness and do anything for her mother. She had done it again tonight, when they had urged her to cut the cake and spend some time with her friends.

Undoubtedly she was the best daughter and wanted the world to know that her father was the best.

She was the best thing to have happened to them. She was the little ray of hope in their otherwise gloomy world. Her bright, blonde hair on top of her head seemed to radiate like a golden halo. Her little, blue eyes sparkled like the waves glistening with sun drops. Her round face with thin pink lips, and her peach tinted cheeks, made her as adorable as her little caring heart.

He wondered how she could regard him as the best father while he had so many shortcomings and flaws.

He was now closer to the house. The little falling place he called home was away from the rest of the town of Turtisvelle. Alone and unused it lay. The rent had been less, so they had chosen it. The local buses were used for commuting to work and school. In the darkness, as the moon threw down its light, the shambles could be seen like an old rotten shed. Helplessness makes man look at the darkest corner with hope. From the porch, he could always see her room, and find her sitting there waiting for him.

Today, it was the same. Though it was late in the night yet the light in the kitchen meant that Sophie was working there. Probably cleaning over the mess the children had left after the party.

Under the radiance of the moon and the street light, he raised his head. His eyes reached the window pane of her room. There she was, sitting sadly, near the window. She sat there waiting for him like every day.

She seemed to look at the lights but her mind was elsewhere. He entered the house and found the hall was all cleaned up. The streamers hung from the ceiling, across the walls, hiding their crumbling walls and faded wallpaper. A tinkling sound of glass from the kitchen indicated that Sophie was washing the dishes.

"You must be very tired," she said turning over to face him.

A slow and soft smile was on her face. She asked him to freshen up while she heated up dinner.

"Hmmm. Sarah?" he mumbled.

"In her room," she informed and turned back to her washing.

Matthew hung the jacket and walked quietly to her room. He knocked the door lightly and turned the doorknob. When his eyes reached her he saw her sitting sadly. The next moment, she looked at him. Those innocent eyes glowed with joy for a second to see him, and instantly became sad again. She glanced at the bag in his hand. He didn't want to give her the gift like this. He entered the room and sat beside her. She was still wearing the bright red dress, with layers of frills. Little sequins of red glittered as the light fell on them. Short balloon sleeves puffed around her slender arms and gave her the royal princess' look.

"Happy birthday princess," he said and kissed her forehead.

"Hmmmmm," she murmured.

"Is my princess.... angry?" he fumbled with his words.

"Mmmm."

She frowned and grumbled. Her eyes went back on the lights outside. The place was still decorated with the town waiting for Christmas, which was two days later.

"Do you want to go out and see those lights?" he asked her.

"No. You must be tired. You should rest," she replied in a soft tone. She was the ever-concerned daughter; pain and sadness were loaded in her voice.

"Naah! I am not tired. My princess needs to see those lights. C'mon let's go."

He pulled her off the bed and quickly picked the red woollen cap and placed it on her little head. She tightened the red muffler across her neck.

Quietly they walked out. Sophie bade them farewell at the door. She was always the soft and strong support of Mathew. She was just two months away from the arrival of the second child. She was the pillar who helped Matthew bear the things they had faced. Be it loss of jobs, financial crisis, or any other situation, Sophie never complained and Matthew only wished he could fulfill every dream of hers. Someday, he would do it.

He walked out of the house with the bag in his hand. They walked till the middle of the street. It was all brightly lit up beyond the turn of the square. He selected a bench by the side, and both of them sat down. About fifteen steps ahead was the fountain. Spruced up with colors, the fountain gushed with water and went silent every few seconds.

He finally decided to give the bag with the gift to her.

"What is this Dad?" she asked confused. It was quite a big box.

"It is for you honey," he said.

"I don't want it. It must be expensive. You shouldn't have bought it Dad," she said in her sweet voice.

"You always wanted one Sarah. Open it. See how lovely she is!" He pushed the box again in her hands.

"No, Dad. I don't want it. I only wanted you to be there. You should have come on time. I wanted that," her voice quivered.

She got up and moved away. He sat there quietly. He had hurt her - hurt her badly. She stood a little far from him, closer to the fountain. She started walking around it, trying to get some distance between them. His eyes got moist. She was the best daughter but he wasn't the best dad for her. He tried, but things always went haywire. She walked ahead and stood on the opposite side of the fountain. She seemed to be enraptured by the beauty of the lights and the water. Yet, there was no emotion that could hide the pain in her eyes.

"Hey sweetheart!" Sarah heard a voice call her name. She slowly raised her head. Standing before her was a young woman, probably in her mid-twenties. How pretty she was! Her eyes had the depth that Sarah often found in her mother's. In her hand were long threads, curled around the fingers. On their ends they had bright, coloured balloons. They were red and blue, yellow and pink, swaying with the wind.

"Hi!" Sarah replied.

"You look so beautiful in this red dress," the young lady said.

"Gee… Thanks! Dad had got it for me, for my birthday," Sarah said with a sad smile. "Which he missed," she said softly to herself. Anger and sadness was evident in her tone.

"Oh! It is your big day then, sweet princess." Her voice was filled with joy.

Sarah looked at her and noticed how different she was. Happiness exuded from her like fragrance from a flower. Her smile was contagious and Sarah felt the smile mirroring on her own face, involuntarily.

"Then, why are you so sad? Don't you think you should be with your Dad now?" she asked Sarah pointing towards Matthew.

"I'm angry at him. He missed my birthday. He was at work while I kept waiting for him," Sarah complained. She paused for a moment to breathe but something struck her.

"How did you know he is my Dad?" Sarah asked suddenly.

"His eyes are on you. He is afraid that you're talking to a stranger – that is me - all alone. He is sad about it too Sarah," she said.

"You know my name also? Who are you? Mom says I shouldn't talk to strangers," Sarah blurted out hurriedly.

"Mom is right. Don't worry. I am not going to harm you. Yes, dear, I know your name."

"But… how do you know my name?"

"Do you really want to know it Sarah?"

"Uhh…. uh!"

"Well it is something like this. Your father was at the store where the crowd was busy in the Christmas and Thanksgiving shopping. I was in there too; trying to get through the queue, past the ocean of men and women, to the cash counter.

Suddenly I saw a little girl, like you. She was dressed in old clothes and a jacket whose colour had faded and it was all worn out. Her little thumbs peeked out from her shoes. She kept saying to herself, 'David will love it' as she walked through the chocolates and confectionery section.

She would lift one box of chocolates from the section and her eyes moved to a corner of the shop across the glass walls. There was David. He was a little boy, younger than her, his nose was pink with the cold outside. He was dressed as shabbily as the girl, while he kept peeping through the glass, eyeing his sister.

He would nod at her. She glanced at the price tag and then put it down. She would move her head left and right to disagree with him. She was out there to buy something for her brother.

She finally picked up a box of chocolates and thoughtfully, started walking towards the salesgirl there. She told her that she had two dollars and the box she picked up was of five. The girl rudely told her to keep it back and buy something that was in her range. Sadness filled her face.

She looked here and there and started walking towards the shelf to keep it back. Unknown to her, someone was watching her keenly. He was near the shelf. He looked at her and smiled. Seeing the pain in her eyes, he bent down to her, and asked her if he could help her.

She repeated the same thing. She wanted the chocolates for David. This time she pointed towards the boy outside, who was trying hard to see through the glass.

Hesitantly, she asked if she could take some of them at least for her kid brother for the two dollars she had. He looked at her and opened his mouth to say something. Even before hearing his voice, she replaced the box in the shelf. She was dejected and started walking away.

Suddenly, he stopped her and said that she could take the whole box as it was on sale. He took the money from her and handed the box to her. He took her to the cashier and asked him to make her bill first. He put his hand into the pocket of his trousers and gave out the money. The box of chocolates was placed in the paper bag.

The man at the cash counter obliged and in a couple of minutes, the girl walked off with the chocolate box in a paper cover, and a radiant smile across her face. She quickly walked out of the shop. I saw her reach little David and hand it over to him. The little boy squealed in delight. She said something to him and pointed at the salesman who had helped her. Both of them waved their tiny hands at him beaming with smiles and started walking away.

Those children were so happy Sarah. I kept observing this and was moved when the man's eyes became moist at the corners. He had paid the remaining three dollars from his pocket. He had worked a little longer to compensate it.

Do you want to know what he said to himself? He said, 'Sarah I am sorry dear, but I don't want another princess to be sad on my princess' birthday'."

Sarah was shocked. She looked at her father and her eyes were filled with tears. He looked back at her. She could see his eyes glimmering with the moisture of his tears, as the lights fell on them.

"That was my dad?" she asked to confirm her thought.

The woman nodded her head in affirmation.

Sarah turned over to look at her father again. Then she looked back at the stranger, speechless. Finally, after a couple of silent minutes, she managed to speak, "Thanks. Thank you so much dear friend. I will never ever be angry on Dad. He is the best, right?" The unknown woman smiled back at Sarah and said, "If you think he is, then he surely is!"

"But ....," she struggled to say more, "how do I make him happy now?"

Smiling innocently, the young woman pulled out a yellow balloon from her bunch and stretched it across for Sarah.

"Take this balloon dear. He will be happy to get it from you. You mean a lot to him. You know that, right?"

She handed Sarah a big yellow one with some strokes of black.

Matthew silently sat there. He was dejected and wondered how he would make his daughter happy again. He had been watching the young stranger talk to his little daughter. She had turned and looked at him, but why were there tears in his princess' eyes? Did that girl say something to her?

Worried by these thoughts, he started to rise. He saw the stranger hand over a balloon to Sarah. He quickly got up. It worried him why the woman was speaking to Sarah. He took a few steps. It surprised him more when he saw Sarah turn and walk towards him; rather she started running towards him with the balloon.

She raced against the air. Instinctively, his arms opened for her and he bent down to hold her. She jumped into his arms. Holding her tight, he tried to balance himself.

"Princess, are you alright?" he asked, really concerned now.

"Yes Dad, I am fine and I am so happy and proud of you!" she said with wet eyes and kissed him on the cheeks. "Dad, you are the best! Do you know that?" she exclaimed looking at him with all the love she had for him.

"No sweetheart. The only thing I know is that, you are the best daughter," he said as he kissed her softly on her forehead.

"Happy birthday baby!" he wished her while he slowly put her down.

"What's this balloon for, dear?" he asked Sarah as he rose to stand.

"Oh! It's for you, Dad," she said and gave it to him.

Matthew's eyes welled up as he read the words those strokes made.

On the yellow balloon, with black glittery strokes was written,

For,

The best Dad

And

Human!

He looked ahead, and walking in the opposite direction was the girl who had spoken to Sarah. He had seen her earlier, probably at the shop. She had smiled that time too just like she was smiling back at him now.

At the store.

Sale.

Chocolate girl.

David.

$2.

$5.

It all raced through his mind. He acknowledged her presence with a nod. She smiled and nodded back, just like she had done at the store.

Clutching the delicate strings of her colourful balloons, she walked away.

Perhaps to another person who needed her. She had to be at the right place for the right person to make them see the right thing. She had a role to play, for she was....**The Balloon Girl.**

Last Promise

Sometimes it is extremely difficult to find a ray of hope when darkness seems to have engulfed you. It envelops you leaving you helpless and in ruins. It leaves you wounded, so badly that you wonder if you could get up, rise up from the ashes and walk again. You wonder if flying is even an imaginable feat.

With these thoughts running in my mind, today I walk ahead, feet laden with heaviness. For it would be nearly impossible to bring in any ray of hope for the person, I had to meet.

"Mrs. Khan, we request you to stay out. Please. It is important for the patient's safety."

I was aghast when the doctors told me that dreadful news an hour ago. Whenever I was found inside the ICU, they would pull me out. They'd separate me from him.

They had used all options and finally declared ruthlessly that Reyhan was sinking. There was nothing they could do about him now. There was not even a ray of hope to hold on to. I was shattered. The broken pieces of my heart and soul were stuck within me and they hurt me more. Nothing hurts more than a mother seeing her child breathe his last, just before her eyes.

I looked through the glass door of the ICU. There he lay asleep. Those little hands pale with green and blue veins protruding, the tubes and needles piercing through the delicate skin. Blood smeared on the bandage tied around his little head. The innocent eyes closed under those thick eye lashes. His thin lips had turned bluish, dried up like severe frostbites. The soft skin which I wasn't allowed to touch, told me to come close and comfort my little angel.

The serenity inside was torturous. The undeterred buzzing of machines around him and the unperturbed movement of nurses and doctors in and out, was adding to my frenzy. I never knew if he was sleeping or unconscious. Or......?

I knew only a few things. I knew that I wasn't ready to lose him. I knew that my eyes were uncontrollably swelling up with tears every moment that passed. I knew I had to forestall this event, but how impossible that was. I couldn't believe that Reyhan, the precious love of my life, my only ray of hope and survival in this world, was a guest on this planet for a few hours, not more.

A rash driver had not seen my little boy and struck him. That selfish and heartless coward did not bother to bring my baby to the hospital. He was left there on the road to bleed. Who was he? I would never know. With the kind of corruption in this rich man's world, I would never be able to know him or punish him for this. Maybe, just maybe, if he was brought on time, Reyhan's life would have been saved. Maybe then he would have got back into my arms, my caring embrace and loving hug.

"Sofia!" I heard someone call out my name softly and a hand touched my shoulder. I looked up.

It was Salim. I had always kept waiting for this man in my life. Today when I saw him, I felt nothing but dislike. Contempt.

Never had I complained about anything to this man. Never had I expected anything from him. Never had I asked him for anything, at least not for myself.

He was equally in pain, but I had no feelings of pity for him. Rather I had no feelings for him at all. Suddenly he felt so distant, like a stranger for me. He always had priorities and we weren't in them. Reyhan and I had always been alone. The little boy had always wanted his Dad. He wasn't there with me or with Reyhan, while we waited for him always.

Now when he finally came unexpectedly and without being called, it was too late.

He came to see Reyhan in this state, not when he came into this world, not when his eyes beamed on seeing me. He wasn't there when Reyhan had started rolling on his back, nor when he crawled for the toy cars. He wasn't there when Reyhan took his first steps. He wasn't there when he spoke the first words.

The first word he uttered was 'Maa.' How wonderful it was to hear it from his soft and naughty lips! The father wasn't there when he had breathed his first in this world. Yet today he was there to be with him. To see him, breathe his last.

Every year he came for a month, to spend a vacation with us. We were just an occasional annual destination for him. With loans and responsibilities on him, I was expected to sacrifice everything and support his decisions. I did them religiously, especially after he gave me the best reason to live, my son Reyhan.

This time when I called, I didn't tell him to come. Still he came when I told him, that our five-year-old son had met with an accident.

Reyhan was the reason that I endured Salim and his absence. Today, I had nothing for him. As every moment passed, Reyhan was taking me and my feelings with him. I didn't want to see the face of that man, who never lived with Reyhan. His tears and sadness looked like pretense. What did he know about my son, to grieve for him! Who was he except for being a biological father!

I pushed away his hand and strode away. Trying to balance myself, I raced down the stairs. I wanted to go away to a silent place, away from this quicksand which seemed keen to pull away my son's breath while I watched helplessly.

I wanted to go with him. I wanted to stop breathing when he stopped. I was crying, desperately. I have never been a loud crier so I needed to move out. Maybe then I could breathe. I stepped out and sat on the metal bench outside the hospital.

My eyes started pouring all over again, as though the floodgates had been opened.

Just then, I felt someone come and sit beside me. I wished it wasn't Salim, because I feared that I would harm him. I was afraid of my anger devouring the patience I had always had.

"Are you alright dear?" that voice asked.

I raised my head, and in that blurred vision, I saw a young girl. She must have been a college girl in early twenties. Her soft pale white skin added a divine radiance to her and the surroundings. She had a small bag on her shoulder which she laid down as she settled beside me. She was wearing a white skirt and a white top. White was the color that meant peace. It was also the color of the shroud.

"Why do you cry?" she asked when I hadn't answered her.

I was feeling so helpless and lonely. When she asked me again, I felt all the pain swell up in my heart, waiting to flow off. I just fell into her arms and cried uncontrollably. She moved closer and hugged me tight.

"Don't cry. Don't!" she said feebly.

I cried till my eyes went dry. I don't know how long it took to stop my tears.

"Are you feeling better now?" she asked as she gave me a bottle of water which she pulled out of her bag.

"Yes. Thanks," I replied wiping away the tears and sipping the water.

"Life is very unfair dear. Sometimes it gives you the best things in life and then it decides to take it away, once you've got used to it, once you've fallen in love with it." She started talking as she looked straight ahead.

"My son! My five-year-old son....," my voice quivered again, "he met with an accident."

She took a deep breath as if trying to prepare herself. A lump was forced down her throat.

"Just a matter of time, and he will be gone.... back to the Creator," she was telling me what I already knew and had dreaded with a softness and serenity in her voice as though she knew what it meant to lose someone you love.

"Yes, and I am not prepared to let that happen. I can't bear it. I love him, I will die with him," I cried.

"No one dies unless their time comes. He was a gift from the Lord to you. Now He wants it back. You can do nothing. We just have to accept His decision. He won't burden a soul more than what it can bear."

"It's easier said than done, young lady!" I hissed through my teeth. What did she know about my pain?

"I know," she replied in her calm voice.

Anger boiled in me when anyone tried to console me with words that were so void of feelings. I erupted from within to hear those words. It was always easy to preach, unless you are in the other person's shoes.

As moments passed, my breathing stabilized and my heart wished for things. I have no idea why but I wanted to share those thoughts with her. She sat beside me, looking at the people moving around.

"If only for some time, I could see my Reyhan, as he always was. Smiling and awake." Hope and wishes that were within me escaped my lips as words.

"Hmmm." She sat back, in a reflective stillness.

"I want you to promise me something," she suddenly spoke breaking her silence.

Seeing the dazed expression on my face, she went on.

"I want you to step out of this. I want you to use your gentleness, your feelings and warmth to spread happiness around. Will you care for those whom even He seems to have left? Will you give the love you have for Reyhan to those desolate and abandoned children?"

I looked up at her. How did she know, that I always felt that life was unfair to those homeless and deserted children! How did she know I ached to run a home for the destitute? How being an orphan had always made me feel for the helpless children who had been left alone in the treacherous world! How I wanted to be a helping hand to the abandoned!

"I know you wanted to do that always," she spoke again making me wonder how she could read my mind. She slowly continued, "Sadly, you'll lose yours, but you will have to accept others'. You can do it. Please don't refuse."

She was requesting me. I was confused by her words.

I reflected over her words. The thought of spending his last few moments with smiles and happiness made it easier for me to decide.

Was a give and take possible here?

"His last moments peacefully with us, and I promise I will do that," I replied.

"Now your turn," she said and looked up at the sky as though telling something to someone up there who was listening to us.

She looked down at me and smiled, "Deal then?"

"Yes," I replied.

She handed me some colorful balloons which she had tied to the bench while we were speaking. I didn't see them, unless she started untying them. She handed them to me and said, "Take these. He loves balloons right."

"Yes!" I said and nodded. The talk with her had been different. It felt like an old connection and strange that she knew all.

"How did you know?" I asked.

Before she could reply, there was a loud voice calling out my name.

I turned and saw Salim. He shouted out again, "Sofiaaaa! Reyhan is awake. He is asking for you. He is back."

Happiness rushed along with blood in my body. The joy of seeing my son as he opens his eyes and looks at me re-energized my soul and body. I got up from the bench and rushed towards the hospital door filled with ecstasy. As I stretched my hand to push the glass door open, it hit me like a dart.

It really was a deal.

He was back for some time. That's what I had wished for. Now I had to make use of the time I had got. I wanted to make his last moments memorable. Garner memories with him. I stood up and looked for her. She had already risen and was walking away.

In her thin hands, she was holding a blue balloon. Something was written on it. As the tear fell from my eye and cleared my vision I could read what was written on it. It was a message.

A message for me:

Keep your promise.

Tears fell as I blinked. Firm in my thoughts and decision, I shouted out, "I will. I will." As loud as I could, I shouted, "Thanks! Thank you....," I didn't know what to call her. Finally, I called out, "Thank you, balloon girl!"

She turned and smiled. She slowly waved her hand and kept walking ahead. I rushed in to be with my son for the last few hours he had got. The time we had to live before darkness enveloped us all.

There were balloons, toys, and posters of Mickey Mouse, Donald Duck, and Superman around him. The teddy bears and flowers filled up the room of the little boy. His eyes closed with a smile when he fell asleep, while I saw his mother caress him. She kept ruffling his hair. I was unseen by people who walked in and out of the wards and floors. Suddenly I saw the mother's fingers stop.

I knew what I was going to see now. I saw a little light fly away, skywards. I saw the pure soul leave this land. I saw the teardrop fall from the mother's eye.

Pain is just so ruthless. Life is so unfair.

Yet, I had to walk ahead.

Me and my balloons.

Word of Mouth

She kept walking ahead on a hot summer noon. Her shadow walked with her on the stony pavement. She saw people move quickly towards their workplaces. The lunch time had ended for all these robotic humans, she thought. All in such a hurry that no one noticed her or her brightly colored balloons. She walked ahead humming the song 'Show me the meaning of being lonely'. She still loved that song. Somehow it was apt today. She knew where she had to be next!

Today was just like any other day. A busy schedule and finally it had come to an end. I knew the traffic would increase, so I decided to walk back home. It wasn't too far. There was no need to hurry. David wasn't home.

Just then my phone buzzed: New Message arrived.

I unlocked my phone and checked the inbox. It was from David.

Hi C! Will b home in 1 hr. Dnnr@Food4Seasons. C ya. Luv.

I had about an hour to reach home and get ready. So I took a deep breath and put my phone back into my purse. A few steps ahead I noticed a new bakery. The little shop had been newly white-washed. On the top, over a white banner, was written in dark brown 'Word of Mouth'. The brown reminded me of chocolates. Involuntarily I started to drool.

Two days ago, Lara had told me about it and warned about the sinfully mouthwatering delicacies there. She had a tough time keeping away from it. She was trying to maintain her weight. Contrarily I had no issues, as long as they could make my salivary glands begin working. It's indeed a blessing to have those genes which allow you to eat as much as you want without putting on weight.

The tempting cupcakes and cookies were beckoning me through the glass walls. The door was open and the aroma began to reach my nostrils. Magically their appearance and smell pulled me in like a magnet attracts iron. I stepped inside letting the smell of baked items fill my breath.

Then I saw him.

Wearing a white, chef's apron on his blue jeans and white shirt, he instantly caught my eyes. Thin transparent gloves over his hands, he was calmly designing the icing on the cake. His blue eyes sparkled in the whiteness that surrounded him. He softly took up a piping cone and fitted the nozzle to it. He asked the young man in front of the counter for the message to be written on the cake.

The guy blushed as he said, "I love you."

The blue-eyed man smiled and a dimple formed on his right cheek. His cheekbones seemed to rise higher and the tanned skin glowed with a joy. He was tall, about six feet and broad shouldered. Somehow he did not quite fit in the cake shop due to his appearance. His looks were something like that of a model out of a magazine.

He started writing it down delicately, as though he was using a fine paint brush on a small canvas. His lips softly repeated the letters as his long fingers moved elegantly to imprint the words in pink on the little white cake. I was awestruck. I had never looked at a guy with so much attention. Except David.

Seeing him so immaculately working, was like seeing an artist carve a sculpture with finesse. He finished it and smiled with satisfaction. He looked up at the guy who was so proud of it as if it was his handiwork. Just then his eyes fell on me.

Embarrassed to be caught eyeing him like that, I smiled at him, and he reciprocated. There was a strange thing in his eyes. His blue eyes had a glint of happiness just a moment ago while he worked on the cake. Something in them changed after he had finished his design. They were filled with an unhealed sadness.

That day I ended up buying a few cupcakes and scones for us – David and me. Though David didn't really like cakes and confectioneries, yet I took them for him. Two things I loved, David and baking. When I left the place with my big bags, the blue-eyed baker waved me goodbye.

As I walked back home, I was filled with thoughts of David. He was the man I was in love with. We were in college when we first met. I had just moved away from my parents.

The thought about my parents filled me with sadness. They had been waiting for me to move away, so that they could go ahead with the divorce. Their marriage had been a compromise they made. God knows for whose sake. They often declared that it was for me. The fact was it was no home. It was a house where people lived to fulfill their duties and responsibilities. It was a shelter which was devoid of love. It could never become a home. Home is where love resides, where feelings are taken care of and memories are made and cherished.

When I joined college, away from them at Stradwell, I was lucky to be given the hostel facility by the management due to my good scores at school. There I met David. He was a happy-go-lucky person, fun loving and smart. Girls always tried hard to get his attention, and he enjoyed it nonetheless. I wasn't sure we could even be friends. He was good looking as well as confident while I was an introvert and preferred to keep to my circle of friends.

When at a friend's party we were introduced, sparks started flying. I was sure it was just a small talk and the next day he would forget all about me. Surprisingly, he proved me wrong. We started sharing notes and helped each other in studies. Our little chats became long night talks on phone. The first kiss happened and my world changed. I realized how important love is in life, and how beautiful it is.

We had been a couple since then. Out of college, we were now living in a flat as roommates. We shared the room with another couple. I took up a job at a consulting agency, after my diploma in management. Things seemed to settle down for me.

Sadly, David had trouble getting a job. He wasn't able to get a proper one. It wasn't about being offered the right job, it was his casual behavior. He would join at a place and within a week or fortnight, some issues would crop up. He thought his employers were lucky to have him. He expected them to regard him highly. If anything went against his thoughts, the decision would be made. He'd leave the job outright.

No discussions done, no opinions asked.

I was trying to make things better for us, but sometimes he would get drunk, stay upset and annoyed for being unable to get a high paying job. He would scream and shout if I tried to console him. He would walk in his room and throw things around. The next morning, he would sober up. He'd cry like a baby for things he had said or done last night. I knew he was helpless and I believed that he was trying to do his best for us! So I would forgive him.

Time passed and we were still together. Somehow I knew we were supposed to be together. I felt so. I changed myself for him, but David had remained the same - moody and irresponsible. I knew; or probably I hoped and believed that he loved me and I loved him too.

With these thoughts whirling in my mind, I reached home and got ready for dinner at Food4Seasons, a little restaurant where we usually spent some of our best times. Whenever David wanted to celebrate something, it was our spot. Did he manage to get this job? Had they selected him? She didn't know about the place or the job, he'd just said, 'there's an interview'.

As I sat on the couch, in my black knee length skirt and the white crisp shirt, waiting for him, I picked up a book. When sleep had embraced me in her arms, I didn't realize.

A loud bang of the door woke me from sleep. David entered the house, staggering and mumbling things to himself. He walked towards his room, unaware of me sitting on the couch. With a loud thud, he fell on the bed. When I peeped in, I saw him lying on the bed, face down. Fully dressed and the bottle rolled down the bed and broke. Shattering into small pieces like the little heart of mine.

I raised his feet above and placed him properly on the bed. Removing his shoes and socks, I pulled the comforter and tucked it around him. With a vision blurred by helpless tears, I brushed the glass pieces on the waste tray and dumped them into the garbage bin.

I walked into the bathroom and washed off the makeup from my face. I changed into my night dress. Sleep eluded me, so I walked into the kitchen. The brown paper bags caught my eyes. I took out a blueberry muffin and kept the pot of water on the stove. I needed some warm coffee to soothe my nerves. I sat alone devouring the muffin with black coffee. I sat alone and sad yet enchanted by the taste of those delicacies.

The next morning David told me about the job. I was filled with dread. In the whole world, the job that enticed him, that excited him was a job at the casino. A manager at the casino! Though I did show my displeasure yet I knew it meant nothing as he had his own way of convincing me, saying that it would make him feel confident. He dreamt of meeting some rich financier and getting a loan to start his own business. My pleas fell on deaf ears.

That was the beginning. As days moved, things were getting stranger. Though I wasn't willing to think about it, but everyone around me - our mutual friends and my friend Lara - felt our relationship was undergoing a dark phase. David seemed to drift farther and farther away from me. He was spending less time with me. He always made plans and promises but fulfilled none of them.

Earlier he was willing to do anything for me, but since he started working at the casino, he had changed. He was becoming too ambitious and demanding. His drinking worsened. His habits and behavior, everything was changing.

During this, the only saving point in my life was my new found friendship. Every day, for pastries or croissants, muffins or marshmallows, I visited Word of Mouth. When they started serving the items with coffee, it became my favorite spot.

With my love for baked items ruling my mind and heart, Norman, the blue-eyed cake guy transformed from a cake seller to a friend. Every day he would sit outside the shop and have his coffee with me. We'd talk about the smells and flavourings. Earlier our talks were about little variations he'd made and how they resulted. Slowly as time passed, our talks began to jump on other casual topics. Yet we avoided personal issues. Both of us were not ready to open those boxes.

I was always intrigued by the sadness which enveloped his eyes the moment he was away from the ingredients or was not decorating the cakes. I was aware that it was something very close to his heart, so I didn't know how to make him talk about it. Until one day, when he decided to tell me all by himself.

It was Friday night and I sat sipping my evening coffee at Word of Mouth. Somehow, I felt Norman was quieter that day compared to the other days. He went about handling the customers, writing little notes and messages on cakes, and sipping his coffee. Most of the time his eyes rose towards the sky like he was looking for a particular star in the star studded sky. Whenever I caught his eyes, he would look away with a sad smile.

David had sent a message that there was a party at the casino so he would probably come back by morning. So I was in no hurry to go home. I didn't want to go back into the empty flat, to be all alone.

As I kept watching Norman do his work, the thought got stronger in my mind. I had to ask him. Tonight.

As the clock's hands ticked, the shop's closing time approached. I helped him clear up the counter and set the tables and chairs inside. Somehow it felt good doing those little chores with him. As the last table and chair were brought in, Norman left them unturned. I brought two cups of hot, black coffee and we sat in the silence. Only a dim light inside and the moon shone around us.

"Norman?" I began.

"Yes Claire," he replied, sadness looming in his voice.

"Can I ask you something?" I said as my fingers played around the rim of the cup.

"Hmmm," his sound echoed in the empty dark shop.

"What is it? Why are your eyes extremely sad tonight?" I asked.

He raised his head and looked at me with questioning eyes.

"N. n... nothing," he murmured softly.

I stretched my hand across the table and touched his.

"Norman, we are friends, right?" I asked him.

"Yes Claire. Of course. Rather you are the only person I call as a friend," he said as his eyes deepened with emotions.

"Tell me Norman... Please," I said, hoping he would share his feelings with me now.

Suddenly in that darkness, I saw a tear roll down those blue eyes. He spoke with so much pain that I wished I hadn't asked him about it.

"Everything I have done or will do in my life is because of Emily. She was the lifeline which kept me alive. She gave me dreams and taught me how to work for them. She gave me ambition and guided me to reach for it. When the time came, when our dreams were coming true gradually, she left." His voice quivered, as he took a deep breath and continued, "When I had just found some joy in being alive, life twisted the arm of my fate, and..... took her away."

"I'm sorry, Norman," I stuttered.

"It's not your fault Claire. We were destined to stay together for a predetermined time. Those moments have been the most memorable for me," he spoke sadly.

"Why did she.... ," I hadn't even completed the question when he stopped me, "Oh! No... No! She did not leave me Claire." He stopped and took a deep breath. With more sadness now, he continued, "She left the world. She deprived the world of her existence." His words struck me with pain.

"She died three years ago. I am working on her dreams, our dreams. Word of Mouth was her dream. This place was her wish. I am living her dream." His voice choked.

"You really loved her a lot, didn't you?" I asked him.

"Yes. Emily was everything for me."

"You miss her so much."

"No. I don't miss her, because she is always with me. In spirit she is always beside me. I do miss her physical existence but that's not such a big deal. Right?" With a soft, sad smile he looked around and the talk ended.

That night, walking back home I wondered what things love made people do. On one side were my parents who had made me question if love was something worth living for. They had made me think and feel that life was just phases of compromises.

Then there was Norman and this girl. Three years and he still lived with her memories. He still loved her and was making her dreams come true. That was love, for sure.

When I opened the door to my empty flat, I had a question in my mind.

Which one was mine?

My friendship with Norman blossomed. The respect I had for him rose to a new level. I started to hope, that one day, David would love me too, like this.

Things between us - David and me - changed a lot as we celebrated our fifth anniversary of being together. He became more aggressive, dominant and pessimistic. I had stopped suggesting or asking things that would aggravate his anger. However hard I tried, he wasn't letting things change for good.

Hell broke loose for me when one day, I saw a pouch of white powder in his pocket. I confronted him. First he denied carrying such a thing in his jacket. When I brought it out to him, he fumbled and started trembling. He tried to convince me it was not his. He had been asked to keep it by a friend. He swore that he wasn't using it.

I realized what was happening. I had to wake up to reality. He was drifting away. Deep in my heart, I felt I had to be with him. He needed me. May be some day, for my sake, he would make an attempt to change, though it seemed to become an impossible mission with each passing day. Was it love between us? Was I just lugging the log believing it to be love?

A couple of months passed. Walls between David and me would rise and fall. While the friendship between Norman and me, was getting stronger. We spoke about family and work. We enjoyed talking about books, cakes, dreams, and other things. David was always in my mind, like a worry, except when I was with Norman. I totally forgot to tell Norman about David. Or did I intentionally avoid it?

Fridays were spent in devouring the mouthwatering things at Word of Mouth, while Saturdays and Sundays went in experimenting what I had learnt about the art of baking from Norman. Slowly I was picking up the little details. I enjoyed every moment I spent there, with Norman. Slowly I felt, the sadness in his eyes had left. There was a new glow in them. They showed that things were changing for Norman.

One Friday nearly a year after the day I had met Norman, things between us took a turn. I was a little late and Norman had got restless. He messaged me, asking my whereabouts. That was something he had never done. Though we had exchanged our numbers earlier, I was always the first one to send a message. Today, something was different. When I reached there, he said he had something important to tell me. After I had my cup of coffee, with cookies filled with vanilla cream, I asked him about it.

What came next left me in shock!

Norman presented a little muffin in front of me. It had pink powdered sugar. With the blue like the color of his eyes, was written with icing, "Will you marry me?"

I was taken aback by his assumption that I was in love with him or would marry him. I didn't know how to react. He was a man whom any girl would be lucky to have. He was an ideal lover and life partner. I was happy when I was in his company. I looked forward to spend my time with him at Word of Mouth. I admired Norman. However, was I in love with him?

I was in love with David, wasn't I?

Was I?

What was I to do?

I was confused but I could not say a yes to Norman. I felt it was wrong of him to think that way, he was a friend. Just a friend. Maybe more than that, a special friend. As I wasn't ready with an answer, I told him I told him about David and me. He listened carefully and I saw his expressions change slowly. All through the words, I later recollected, I stressed on 'staying there for David', insisting that 'David needed me', but not once did I tell him that I loved David. It was something that surprised me. Why didn't I say that?

He heard everything silently. The glow that had started enriching his eyes these days started fading again.

Just then an old woman walked in. He rose to attend to her. He walked a step away and turned back to face me. "I knew this would happen. Destiny can't be so kind to me. I shouldn't have asked you. I did it because Emily told me last night that I should."

I was shocked. Emily was his girlfriend - his dead girlfriend. He always said he felt she was still guiding him. Was she guiding him to me? Or was she guiding me to him?

I waited, hoping to speak to him again. He stayed away for the next hour that I spent there. I knew he would never want to see me anymore. Without causing more pain and agony to him, I walked out of the cake shop. More agonized than ever.

Three months passed after that incident in the cake shop. Things were still the same physically but somehow deep in me, a lot had changed. Now I could never walk into that shop like I did earlier. I always hid and stole glimpses of Norman from the glass window when he wasn't watching. I saw his eyes carry the same sadness which I had seen earlier.

Like every day, for the last three months, I have been sitting on the bench on the opposite road, in a spot invisible from Word of Mouth. I don't have the courage to go and talk to Norman again, but I can't let a day pass without seeing him. His blue eyes – sad and blue eyes.

Little did I know that today things would change…

"Hey dear, can I join you?" I heard the soft voice of a young girl.

Dressed in blue jeans and wearing a yellow floral tee shirt, she looked like a girl on the way to her college. She had a few balloons in her hand.

"Sure," I said and she smiled back. What a sweet smile she had!

She sat quietly, looking past the balloons. I wondered if there was some party going around.

"You look sad. What happened?" she asked.

Something in her eyes worked like a spell. I wanted to tell her everything, everything that I was unable to tell anyone. I wanted to open my heart and its wounds to her.

"I don't know. I am confused," I replied truthfully as my eyes turned towards Norman again.

"It happens when you try to find love where it doesn't exist. You push away love while it keeps waiting for you."

Her remark shook me. I looked at her, amazed at her statement.

"You are waiting for love to radiate from that corner where it doesn't even exist. In doing that, you are letting go of the love which only a few are able to get." Her words surprised me further.

"Stop looking at me like that. Tell me all. Maybe I can be of some help," she said innocently.

I told her everything. After she heard my story, she asked me something that hit me like a bolt.

"Are you happy with David? Do you love him? Or are Norman's eyes in your mind?"

"I don't know," I replied, more confused.

"Let's make it clearer for you then," she said.

"See those flowers?" she asked, pointing at the flower shop nearby.

"Hmmm," I replied.

"See these balloons?"

"Oh yes! I see them."

"Now, close your eyes. Trust me, just close your eyes. In that darkness under your eyes now, can you see the soft light around?"

I closed my eyes. There was nothing but an eerie darkness.

"No, I don't see anything," I said and my eyelashes fluttered as I opened my eyes.

"Please, just try it with your heart and soul, you will see it."

Slowly she placed her soft hands on my eyes, closing my eyes. She kept on talking to me while I sat still.

"You see the light illuminating the darkness away."

"Mmmm," I replied after a few moments, for a white ray of light emerged in the darkness of my covered eyes.

"Good! Now, recollect those flowers, those pink, red, yellow, white, beautiful and colorful flowers."

"Hmmmmm."

"Now, you see the brightly colored balloons; of different sizes and shapes and colors. They are all coming in your view."

"Yes, I see them," I said, thrilled to be able to see things with eyes closed.

"Now, can you see a face among those balloons? See carefully, somewhere at the back, among those bright balloons and soft tender flowers. Can you see him?"

I tried and tried, there was nothing. Then, it happened. I did see a face. With a sudden jerk, as though a sudden revelation was granted to me, I opened my eyes.

She was nowhere to be seen, but I knew what I had seen.

Things between David and me had been deteriorating. Lately he was avoiding me totally. He didn't pick my calls, or reply to my messages. He left before I returned home. He came after I left for office. I was worried for him, I cared for him, but I had doubts about the fact that I loved him. Today the girl had cleared my mind. I knew what I had to do.

I started walking towards Word of Mouth, towards Norman. Just before I stepped in, I saw a reflection in the glass door of the shop. The girl was standing behind me. She was on the other side of the road, holding her bright balloons. I turned to see her. She smiled at me and sent a white balloon flying in the sky. I raised my head, and words were written on it.

He'll love you always!

Go for it!

In bright red, the message was written on the balloons. I looked at it and smiled. I lowered my head to where she was standing, but she had vanished in thin air again.

I was on the threshold of my new life, where love awaited me. I stepped inside into the familiar aroma of cakes, sweets and baked food, and the warmth of Norman came rushing towards me, waiting to embrace me. His blue eyes regaining that sparkle slowly, as though he knew what my approaching steps meant.

Those shining eyes told me he was ready to take me back. I had been blind to the fact that I was in love with him. All the time I wanted to be loved in return by someone. When love came to me I was turning a blind eye to it.

In the reflection on the glass walls as I bake and decorate the cakes with Norman, I often see the balloons and peep out to see if she would come visiting again. She, who cleared the haze in my mind, and made me step into the world of love, she whom I call....

The Balloon Girl!

Aliyaa

In the scorching heat, on the dried parched land, my steps took me into a new horizon. I wasn't even aware who needed me now? Whose life was I to step in and out? Where do you stand Aliyaa? As these thoughts rushed in my mind, the people rushed on their terraces, long kurtas (tunics) and long scarves or skullcaps covering their head. Suddenly they all started greeting each other after sighting the crescent in the sky. The blessed month of Ramadan was here. I was going to be part of Aliyaa's story.

Times are so difficult sometimes for some people. Festivals bring in happiness in few homes, while for the others they bring in the feeling of helplessness and dejection, the feeling of falling short in front of others, specially their own children.

Children make you feel so helpless when they ask you for things which are far beyond your reach. They make wishes and hope that their mother will fulfill them as though she is a superwoman or a fairy of the tales they hear and read as they grow up.

Something like this was on my mind, throughout the month of Ramadan.

You might be wondering who I am. Well, I am Aliyaa.

It was the 29th day of Ramadhan. Washing the dishes, I was lost in my thoughts. Most of the dishes were of crystal glass, some brand Bibi ji said which I always found difficult to pronounce or remember.

How was I going to tell the children?

What would I take home for them?

"Aliyaaaaa! How many times should I tell you to be careful when you wash the dishes?" Bibi ji's voice resonated in the kitchen and brought me out of the mental distress.

"Sorry Bibi ji. Nothing broke. I will be careful now. Just a little tension at home," I tried to convince Bibi ji.

"Always an excuse ready on your lips, eh? Just don't break anything or waste water. Once you are done, I will tell you the things to prepare for Iftar. You know today might be the last day of Ramadan. Sadiya wants it to be a special one," Bibi ji announced leaving the kitchen as she fanned herself with the dupatta (scarf).

Seeing her walk away, I took up the end of the water soaked dupatta and wiped the sweat off my face. I washed my hands clean and wiping them dry, I began to arrange the dishes back into the cabinets. I kept trying as much as possible to keep my wild thoughts in rein.

As the day passed, I had completed all the work. The cleaning and washing was done. Bibi ji always started the preparations a day earlier; it wouldn't be a problem if the announcement of Eid came sooner or later. It also helped me as the work was properly completed and I was allowed to leave early. Each time I tried to drive away those thoughts, those innocent, questioning faces flashed in my mind. Questions which I couldn't answer!

There's nothing worse than helplessness in the world.

As time neared, worry kept on creeping within me. I tried to keep my personal problems and thoughts at bay. I fried the samosas and the rolls. I had made the fruit salad, Sadiya bibi's favourite. Calmly, I prepared the tangy chole just like Sahab ji liked and was only left with the task to fry the puris.

I always felt a smile spring on my face when I made something for Sadiya bibi. She was the most adorable child I had ever met. Whenever I did something for her, I did it wholeheartedly.

"Allah, how will I tell them? How shall I even face those innocent eyes?" I kept asking the Lord to provide some answers.

Just then a beggar knocked at the door. Bibi ji called out, "Aliyaa, there's some food in the refrigerator. Stop the man and give him the food. Also add up some fruits from the basket."

"Ji, Bibi ji (Yes, Ma'am)," I replied and hurried to stop the beggar. I called out to him and he had stopped under the shade a few steps farther from the house. I quickly rushed back inside and packed the food and added an apple and an orange in the package. I slipped my feet into the slippers and covering my head with my dupatta I stepped out.

I walked up to the man. He wore all tattered clothes and seemed to be extremely hungry. As soon as he saw the apple, he devoured it wolfishly.

"God bless you!" the old beggar remarked.

"Bless the ones who have sent this food for you. Do remember all in your prayers. Peace and blessings!" I said and started to walk towards the house.

"Peace and blessings on all of us!" A soft sweet voice reached my ears from behind. I suddenly turned as I covered my face with one end of my dupatta.

There stood a young college girl, dressed in white. Her face was radiant and had an innocent charm. Her soft thin lips made her smile so angelic that I wondered if she really was a human or an illusion or a fairy stepping out of the stories I often heard from my children.

Wearing a white long ankle length frock and a red colored dupatta spread over her bosom and covering the blonde hair, she stood a few steps away from me.

"Peace and blessings on you too," I replied and smiled back at her. Her face was so mesmerizing that a smile automatically spread while I watched her.

"Kaise ho aap (How are you?)" she asked.

I was amazed how differently she spoke. She was a foreigner. Her attempts to speak Urdu made me giggle. I had to stuff my dupatta into my mouth to stop myself from laughing.

"Main theek hun, (I am fine)," I replied with a huge grin.

"I came here to visit a friend of mine," she continued to speak in accented Urdu, "Could you show me where the 'Word of Mouth' cake shop is?"

"You have come at the right place madam ji," I replied, glad I could be some help to the foreigner. "It is at the corner, to the left at the end of the street."

"Can you walk along with me till there?" The girl walked closer and held my hands. Somehow I felt a strange connection with her and didn't want to disappoint her. I nodded my head and started walking slowly.

"So, why are you so worried Aliyaa?" she asked.

I was surprised how she knew my name. She must have noticed the shock, for a grin spread on her face as she spoke. "I heard the lady in the house call out and then you stepped out of the house. So I guessed it was your name. Am I right?"

Convinced by her answer, I smiled and nodded my head, "You are right."

When I didn't speak further she asked the same question again. Unknowingly I started telling her my story. I have never been comfortable telling about myself and my life to anyone but today it was different. With this girl, it was different. Why? How? I had no idea but something made me spill out everything to her.

"A few months ago I joined here. A huge palatial home needed a maid and I had been able to please Bibi ji with my hard work and honesty. I am happy working here but the money is spent mostly in making ends meet. After my husband's death, I had a tough time making life livable for myself and two young children. My family had maintained the status quo prevalent in most of the villages in our country. A girl leaves her parent's house in a palanquin and never returns into it unless it is the last ride to the graveyard."

"Further, my in-laws called me a witch, a curse to the family whose ill fate had taken away their son. Even the progeny of their loved son didn't mean anything to them. It was so probably because they had my bad, cursed blood in their body. That's the fate of a woman even today in our society and country. Though the religions don't call upon such discrimination, society does. Soon after widowhood became my destiny, I had to take a friend's help and started working as a maid. I got my children admitted into a small school. With just a meager salary, I was content."

"Allah has been kind. I got to work for good and kind families. I had been working at three homes and was collecting a small amount. My friend told me that the owner of this house wanted a maid fulltime, from 7 am to 6 pm, with more salary than I was already earning, so I decided to take it up."

"It was just six months and Ramadhan stepped in. Ramadhan is a blessing. Meals are forsaken, a date and some items which Bibi ji packs for us is enough for Iftar. I have to cook a little for dinner and Suhur (the pre-dawn meal). However, these last days have been the most difficult to pass. These are the days when the children demand to go shopping. They demand clothes and accessories."

"We are poor but I strive hard to make my children happy. I tried to work more to please the mistress of the houses so that they would give something extra as a gift or bonus. Every year, as everyone has to give their charity to the needy, I get a little more than normal. Zakat is a blessing for the poor like me."

"Bibi ji too had said she would give some things but then she seems to have forgotten. With the wishes of the children lurking in my mind, I feel I should forsake self-respect and remind Bibi ji. Somehow I haven't been able to."

I felt no shame, no regret to tell her how helpless I felt when my children asked me for things. I didn't feel like a low creature when I told her how I awaited the charity, the Zakat from my employers and others to make ends meet. I felt like I was telling all about myself to a long lost friend of mine, someone who wouldn't judge me, someone who wasn't going to gossip.

"Aliyaa sometimes it helps to tell about your pains to someone. Sometimes a stranger can be easier to talk to and share your woes with. Don't worry. Have faith!" The stranger spoke with a peaceful glow on her face.

I looked at her quizzically. I did feel better after I had shared things with her. We had reached the cake shop and I bid her goodbye. She smiled and handed me a packet which had six green balloons. She said the children could blow air into them and play in the evening. Something was written on them with white. I didn't know what it was so I just carried them home. I was going to give a pair to the three angels of my life, my children and Sadiya bibi.

When I arranged all the food on the table and was doing the ablution, I heard Sadiya bibi enter the hall with huge shopping bags.

"Aliyaa di, are you fasting?" she asked innocently.

She was a lovely child - Sadiya bibi. She was loved by all and sometimes would behave as a spoilt brat but she always showed a lot of respect and admiration for me.

"Yes Sadiya bibi," I replied smilingly.

"Woowwww! You seem to have prepared a whole feast," she said beaming with joy as her nose sniffed the aroma of the dishes I had prepared.

A smile spread on my face.

I started wearing my burqa (cloak). Bibi ji entered with the tiffin. She was all picky and haughty but you could never understand Bibi ji. She always packed the Iftar for children and me. She started this after she saw Saniya and Faraz once. They had come when they had a short vacation and insisted to see the place where I worked.

"Aliyaa take this. Every day I should tell you?" she smirked.

I quietly walked up to her and took it.

"Aliyaa di, wait," Sadiya bibi called out and rose from the sofa.

The mother and daughter looked at me and their eyes sparkled. The elder one's eyes had gone soft suddenly while the younger one's eyes were filled with mischief.

"Sadiya bibi, what is it? I should leave else I won't reach home in time for Iftar. Saniya and Faraz will worry," I said.

"Oh! They won't Aliyaa di." She smiled.

"Abbu ji," Sadiya bibi called out.

Sahab ji entered with two little children walking behind him. Oh guests! I thought.

When my eyes reached their faces, a gasp escaped from my lips. My eyes were wide open and confusion filled me.

Standing before me, were my little children.

Dressed in a new pink frock with white flowers and frills, Saniya was confused yet happiness radiated from her. She was holding another bag in her hand. Faraz was wearing a light blue shirt with a nice pair of jeans, jubilantly showing his set of milk teeth. He too had a bag in his hand. They both were wearing new dresses - the ones which they had shown me when we had crossed the markets last week. They had wanted those for Eid.

"Sahab ji? Bibi ji?" Those words were what I could utter in that dazed state. Tears flowed from my eyes.

I had no money to get them dresses. I had no words to tell them about my inability to buy those dresses for them. But now they stood before me, wearing them already.

Bibj ji walked towards me. She put her hand on my shoulder, "Aliyaa, you did never tell us nor did you ever ask. Neither did it cross my mind that I had forgotten about giving you what I had promised. But someone reminded me and said that I should now give you what I promised as well something more for your patience and self-respect."

Even before anyone could tell me, I knew who that someone was. It was Sadiya bibi. She was the little girl who was always kind to me. She was like my own Saniya, just a little older.

I looked at her with tears blurring my vision, Sadiya bibi's eyes filled up too.

"Aliyaa di, how could I leave you while I did my Eid preparations? Unless we give your share to you, our Eid will not be blessed by Allah. Now, now, don't cry," she said as she walked close to Aliyaa's children.

"Ammi, Abbu, let's sit for Iftar now. Today I have my own guests," she said and pulled along Sadiya and Faraz with her. Bibi ji pulled me along as she kept wiping her eyes.

With all happiness and gratitude filled in my heart, prayers spluttering from my lips, I sat with them.

Together they sat to break the last fast of the month. They celebrated together the sighting of the moon and the preparations of Eid. As I handed over the balloons to the children, they joyously blew air in them and let them fly upwards, towards the sky. Watching the events that had passed in the last few hours I was left with words of that young girl I had me today. How true the words were!

We just need to have a little faith and things happen when you least expect them to happen. As my eyes moved down from the sky towards the corner of the street, I saw the young girl I met in the morning. She stood there holding more balloons. They were all white and Sadiya bibi told me they had "Eid Mubarak!" written on them. Slowly one by one, she was releasing them and they all flew up, making the sky colorful and spreading smiles and keeping faith alive in the hearts of the ones who saw them rise.

For first time in years, Aliyaa was ecstatic and overjoyed seeing the happiness on the faces of the three angels in her life. Her children - Saniya and Faraz- and Sadiya.

Far across her, was the girl who began to walk again. To a new place and to new people she went. The one whom all heard of, yet no one knew at all.......

The Balloon Girl.

A Son's Vow

Sometimes what you vow never to do in life, you end up getting into it, unknowingly. Something like that was happening somewhere and I was needed there. Walking on the stony footpath, I knew I had to be there in time, else not just a person but a whole family would be broken. I couldn't let that happen, just because of a small mistake. I couldn't let him down now when he would stumble on his path.

The little food we had had for breakfast was meager by all means but we weren't supposed to have complaints about it. Life was unjust in so many ways. It was unfair to many of us. I realized this very soon in life. With mother working as a maid, scrubbing floors and utensils with her hands, I knew life was always going to throw bricks at us while we tried to survive safely.

"Mother has already left. Let's clean up the plates and leave for school," I announced to the sleepy heads who were chewing food lazily.

Kiran and Jyothi were my younger siblings, who kept moaning and grumbling while they got ready to go to school. They knew I would pull and drag them yet they would groan every day about it. They did all their acts and pretensions after mother had gone. She never knew how devilishly they behaved behind her back.

After father's death, mother had to single handedly manage everything for us. It wasn't new for her, for she was doing it even when he was alive. I always believed she was rather relieved when he died. At least now she was not subjected to his cruelty.

Every day we saw our father consume alcohol. He'd then come and ask her for money for gambling and drinks. When she didn't hand it over to him, explaining that they were already paid as school fees or for books or food, he would beat her up with anything he could lay his hands on.

Make those bastards work. Why do they need to study?

Send them to work not school.

Give me that money, I will bring back double of it.

Every day he shouted a different line. When mother wouldn't relent, he would slap her, kick her and hit her till his hands would fall tired.

"Deepak, take Kiran and Jyoti outside and play," she would tell when he began his screams. She always tried to keep us away from him in his drunken state. Men do the scariest things under the spell of alcohol.

She never allowed us to witness anything. She never wanted us to know. As the eldest one, I knew. I saw the blood she spitted when she gargled, hours after she had been struck. I saw those blue-black hued arms and legs of hers, which she covered up with her sari. I saw the tears that fell from her eyes, when she thought we were asleep.

I saw everything and every night I resolved to be a better man and son, not what my father was. I wanted to be like my mother. One who was hardworking, caring, loving, and strong. Father was a weak man. After he lost his job, every morning he would go looking for another work. When he would be rejected or disappointed by the wages or wasn't happy with the work, he drank and gambled. All in frustration, he said. This happened often and we ended up slipping deeper into the trails of poverty.

Mother tried to keep his spirits up, but in vain. He was weak-willed and that led to tougher times for her. When one night he didn't return, I was surprised to see her so worried.

I thought mother was mad. She loved and cared for that man who was so violent and reckless towards all of us. It was by midnight when we came to know, that he had been hit by a speeding car near the pavement, where he lay down, heavily drunk. His friends brought home his body, dead.

Time after that did change. It was peaceful now. There was no more violence she was subjected to. Life was smoother than before but still a huge mountainous ordeal for us. Money was always lesser in supply than the demand. Food, rent, medicines whenever someone fell sick and education, the expenses would always keep mother restless.

As mother's earnings weren't enough for our increasing expenditure, I took up work at the tea stall near my school. After school, Kiran and Jyoti would return home and I would go to the tea stall and work till 10 in the night. Mother didn't favour my work but I knew she was struggling with the expenses, especially mine as I was now in class 10. More fees and expenditure as it was the Board examinations. I studied whenever I could at the tea stall. After reaching home, I would be too tired to study or play. My earnings helped little but I was happy to do something for mother. Little by little I wanted to reduce the burden destiny had placed on my mother's frail shoulders.

Time flew, like a soaring eagle. Just two months were left for exams. I was preparing well, fully aware that mother's hopes were pinned on me. A good performance ensured that I would be granted some merit scholarship and admission in some good college in the city if I performed exceptionally well.

"Good education for a good future," mother always told me.

When the examinations began, mother and I burnt the midnight oil. She convinced me to stay away from the work I did at the tea stall. She even went and spoke to the owner and he gladly agreed, as he was all praise for me.

"He is indeed a hard worker, like you Maya," he had said and I felt like someone gave me an award. It was a compliment to be compared to mother.

Mother asked the mistress of the house where she worked for an advance, and brought fresh fruits and milk every day. She would stay awake till I studied and help me with whatever I needed. She didn't allow me to even get up for a glass of water. She fanned me for hours whenever there was a power cut. It was common during the summer in the city, rather a common thing in the whole country. The little thatched house we lived in became hotter as the hot wind hit our faces, slapping us with the heat wave.

All her hopes and our future depended on me. I had a huge opportunity to do something for mother and I wanted to make use of it. Fortunately, all the exams passed away smoothly.

I got back to the tea stall for work. Though mother again was against it, I felt it was better than to spend time loitering around with the other boys of the area. Most of them literally disliked me for not playing around in lanes with them. Instead I would spend time studying and their parents would reprimand them and compare.

Their friendship wasn't my goal.

Mother's dreams were.

People's appreciation wasn't my reward.

Mother's smile was.

Mother waited for the results more anxiously than me. Every day, she would go to the temple and pray for my success. She made promises to God that she would offer this and that as sacrifices to appease Him. I always wondered if God would listen. Did he ever listen to her? If he really did, father wouldn't have been that reckless man, nor would he have died. I guess those idols are selective in their hearing of prayers. Would they hear her prayers this time?

When my results were declared, I ran towards the nearest internet access point. A man in his forties seemed to be accessing the website and checking the results of the students who came there. When I asked the man to check my result, he noted down my roll number and entered it in the search box. My heart was beating hard. I wasn't scared of failure. I knew I'd pass through. Passing through wasn't on my mind. I needed a top score. When the man pressed enter and waited for the server to respond, each second seemed to pass like ages.

When a result came forth, he looked at my face and said, "Is it yours?"

"Yes bhaiya ji," I said, "What happened?"

An appreciative smile came on his face and he said, "Congratulations. You got a 97%! I will give you the print out only when you get me some sweets."

My heart did somersaults and started jumping like the Australian kangaroo. All the people around came and shook hands with me.

The man handed me the print out, patted my back as he said, "Go boy. Don't forget to get some sweets for me too. Congratulate your parents. You've made them proud!"

"Maa. Maa." I could only utter that word. She was the one who deserved everything.

I thanked him as I rushed out of the shop and ran towards the house, shouting for mother all along.

My joy and mother's happiness had no limits. I saw mother at home. Clutching the printout of my result in my hand, I fell into her arms and cried. Seeing me sob like that, she was scared, but I couldn't speak. Finally, when I told her my percentage, we both stood in the middle of the room, hugging each other and crying. She took out some money from the knot at the edge of her torn blue cotton sari and gave me.

"Go get sweets and distribute in the whole basti," she said, wiping tears from her cheek with the same corner of the sari which was empty now.

I took the money and got sweets from the sweets shop. First I went to my school and took blessings from my principal and teachers. They were extremely glad and told me that I had topped from the school. It was the first time someone had scored more than 90% from the little government aided school. They were all praises for me and mother.

"It is all because of your mother."

"Her hard work has paid off."

"Make her proud Deepak."

Everyone said.

I was filled with pride for my success and the respect they had for *my mother*.

Next I went to the internet shop and met that man who had told me the result. He gladly took a small piece from the box and wished me luck for my future.

When I had distributed sweets in the basti, my friends tugged along with me and kept asking for a treat. Ignoring them, I went home to give back the remaining money and sweets.

Mother, Kiran and Jyoti ate the sweets and rejoiced. It was our simple celebration. When my friends came at the door and called out for me, mother gave me back the money and said, "Go Deepak, celebrate it my son. You've worked hard for this."

I was uncertain if I should spend that money just like that. Mother would hear no more and pushed me out.

The day was mine. Our good time was going to start. Things were going to change. Now was the chance I had kept waiting for. With my legs unable to stay on the ground, I jumped out to spend the next few hours with my friends and weave new dreams for us.

It was nearly midnight when I returned home. My vision was all hazy and I felt tired and lost. I staggered my way up to the door and knocked softly. I was scared all along the way that I had been out for too long and mother would be angry. My friends consoled me saying she wouldn't, because she herself had asked me to celebrate.

When mother opened the door, I could see worry plastered on her face. For less than a minute it stayed on her face. Then her worry disappeared and a strange emotion filled her eyes and face. It was bewilderment and then anger. I tried to walk inside but she didn't let me in. She held me by the arm. Her grip was tight. Never had mother held me so tightly. Surprised, I raised my eyes to her. There was a tear in her eyes and astonishment on her lovely face. Unsteady and sleepy, I murmured, "What happened, Maa?"

Before I could hear her voice, I felt her hand, warm and hard, strike across my face. A burning fire raged under the skin of my cheek as I touched it with my own hand. For the first time, mother had hit me. She had slapped me. Tears welled up in my eyes.

"Maa," I cried, hurt and confused.

"Get out Deepak," she said softly but firmly and pushed me out.

She closed the door on my face. I was confused and angry. I banged the door and shouted at her. Fearing that everyone would awaken and gather around, I walked away.

A few steps away from the basti, was an old fountain. Its water had dried up long ago. Just the structure stood there, silent and alone. I sat at the edge of it. Alone, like the fountain.

Unable to control my feelings, I burst into tears. I had done everything as she had wanted. Yet she treated me this way. Why? Why did she slap me? I was confused and angered by my mother's behavior.

I didn't know how long I cried. Finally, when no tears fell, I just sat there in solitude and silence.

"Why did you do that Deepak?" I heard a female voice ask.

I lifted my head and rubbed my eyes to see who had spoken. I saw a young woman, older than me but younger than mother, probably in her twenties sitting beside me. Her face had sadness yet she radiated an innocence I had never seen earlier. I felt like she was someone I knew or someone who knew me better. I didn't feel scared like I always did when I was around strangers. There was a familial feeling about her.

"What did I do?" I asked confused, "I just had a good time celebrating my success with my friends. She had said I could go."

"Yes she did ask you to go and celebrate. How did you celebrate Deepak?" She questioned again with concern clear in her voice.

"We had food, went to the park at the corner of the street. We played cricket. We sat in some rides. We roamed around. At the end, we sat in the park talking about what we planned to do in future." I listed out everything to her.

Though she was a stranger, I didn't feel awkward telling her everything.

"Then? Do you remember what you had while you made plans for your future with your friends?" she asked patiently.

Then it struck me. The staggering walk, my unsteadiness. The hazy vision, banging the door and shouting aloud. Mother's anger and baffled eyes. Her slap on my face. I had done what I always hated. I had done what I despised my father for. I had sat there and got drunk with my friends. I didn't know who brought it there. I remembered one of the boys cajoling me to drink some of it.

"It is the way the rich celebrate," he had said.

"Just a little won't make much difference," another had persisted.

"Mother won't even know," the third had said.

71

I had got persuaded into it.

Tears fell from my eyes afresh.

"I didn't do it intentionally, didi," I cried. "I never realized Maa would react like this. She hates me now. She will never forgive me."

She moved closer to me now and slipped her arm across my shoulder.

"Deepak, your mother has gone through a lot. You have always been a silent witness to it. You have seen every trauma and torture she faced. You are a wonderful child, a strong boy. When you achieved success, it was like a gift you gave her. She has immense love for the three of you. She always feels that it is you who will change the future for them. She has seen dreams with open and closed eyes, for you. She is ready to face the world for you all."

"As night passed, she was worried about your safety. She was scared to death. Every minute she spent was in fear, offering prayers for your safety. When you came home drunk, she saw her hopes and dreams fall like a pack of cards. Crumbling and shattering like glass. Her son, who has always been her lifeline, comes home drunk. Just like his father, her husband."

She wiped the tears off my cheek and raised my chin to make my eyes meet hers.

"She loves you more than anything Deepak. Don't break her dreams and hopes. She will die in no time. She lives for you and your siblings. Help her always. I know you can do that. You can! She cannot hate you ever, for she is a mother. She must have already forgiven you."

Just then there was a rustle at the back. I turned and saw mother walking towards me. Her face was pale with worry and tears were streaming down.

I turned back to face the girl, but she was nowhere to be seen.

Mother saw me and started walking in my direction. She stood close to me, while I had my head hanging low, unable to even see her in the eye. She took my hands in hers and pulled me up to stand. She left them as soon as I stood. With a swift movement she turned, with her back towards me. She was trying to hide her tears, I knew that.

"Why did you do this, Deepak?" she asked, sadness looming in her voice.

I flung open my arms and threw myself at her. Encircling my arms across her waist, my face wet with tears drenched her back. I cried in repentance.

"I'm sorry, Maa. I won't do it ever. Never again," I sobbed uncontrollably.

Mother slowly turned and wiped my tears off. She kissed my forehead softly and ruffled my hair like she always did. She held my hand warmly and said, "Let's go home now."

We started to walk back towards home slowly. After a few steps, I turned back. There she was, though a moment ago she had just vanished.

Standing with a little white balloon, with an aura around her, she smiled back at me.

The white balloon flew from her hands and as my eyes followed it I saw something written on it.

You can

Do it!

With a firm resolve to stay away from the poisonous fluid that brought nothing but sadness to our lives; and a determination to do what it takes to make my mother proud of me, to fulfill all her dreams, I walked back home.

I had no idea that the angelic figure whom I met was known to other people like you (the readers), as....**The Balloon Girl.**

Stay in Love

I walked towards her, she needed me. She needed help; a different kind of help. She needed someone to show her how precious it was, what she was driving away. She was pushing away something, which was the most important part of her life. I had to go. I had to be there for her, before all was lost.

I had to!

———————————

It was difficult. Extremely difficult for me and equally terrifying for her.

Her!

She was the woman who meant the world to me. Now she was pushing me out of her world. I couldn't do that. I couldn't let her move me away, just like that. I won't let her do that. Yes. I won't. Come, what may!

I still get goose bumps and my heart beat races when I think of that day. That dreadful day in our lives. I had never imagined even in my dreams, the trauma and pain I had felt that day. It had begun as simple as a silent wave, the routine calls, the everyday rush to work, the 'Hi Honey…Love you' messages. It even was coming to an end on the same casual end, but that wasn't to happen. The turbulent storm hit me when the telephone rang. I was waiting for Diane at dinner. I knew she'd be late to return from her work. We were supposed to have a dinner date.

It was a dinner date, to discuss the plan for the D-day. On the 14th of February, Valentine's Day, we were supposed to get tied up into the blissful bond of marriage. It was 17th of January, when tragedy struck us.

I kept waiting at the restaurant for about an hour, restless and bored. It was something we always argued upon. Diane would get so busy in her work that she would forget about our plans. Sometimes I ended up as the culprit too. I enjoyed the times when she did it, because then she showed more love and did lots of things to appease me.

I had called up many times on her mobile but she didn't receive even one. I sat drinking Coke, when the mobile rang. It was an unknown number. I picked it. A solemn female voice spoke from the other side, but the words which I heard, struck me like lightning.

"Is this Chris?"

"Yes."

"Sir, where are you? Can you reach the City Hospital now?"

"I can, but what's wrong? Who is this?"

"This is an emergency call and I can't give more details. I would request you to come as soon as possible. The patient is in the ICU. Please hurry sir."

"For God's sake, tell me what happened? Please tell me."

"It's Diane. We saw her office ID card and on it the number to contact in case of emergency was yours. Please contact her family too. We need you here *soon*." The stress she put on the word soon was enough to make the ground under my feet shake.

As soon as she disconnected the call, I sat motionless. It all came pouring down on me. That was the reason for her delay. I was waiting to scold and tease her. I picked up my car keys and paid for the Coke. I raced through the traffic. There weren't many cars around and the hospital wasn't far, yet the distance seemed to increase with each passing minute. It felt as though I was travelling to the other side of the globe. Finally, I managed to reach the Hospital; it had barely taken fifteen minutes. I rushed inside and asked for the ICU.

Please God! Oh! Please.

When I stepped near the glass walls of the ICU, my knees weakened and I leaned onto the wall to stop myself from collapsing there. Seeing Diane, with blood on her beautiful face and her tender body lying on the bed, showing no movement, gave me shivers.

I couldn't be such an unlucky fool to lose the love of my life like this. I couldn't even think of living away from her. To imagine a life without her presence was something I had never even dreamt of.

The machines inside were beeping and the tiny lights kept fluctuating, while the crowd of doctors and nurses was hovering around her. I wanted to get in. No one allowed me. Finally, one of the nurses, a woman who seemed to have understood my pain gave me a comforting look from within the ICU. The caring and understanding face stepped out and asked, "Are you Chris?"

"Yes. I am Chris. I had received the call."

"I was the one who called you."

"What happened? How is she?"

"She was hit by a car. We don't know the details but the driver of the other car died instantly. He was hit badly and the shock led to cardiac arrest."

I dreading asking it but I had to, "How is she?"

"She is in a critical position. There has been severe blood loss and the impact of the blow has been huge. We are trying our best. You should keep patience and pray, my boy."

Saying those words, she patted on my shoulder and walked away. I sat there on the bench, helpless and worried. Scared and scarred. My eyes welled up as I glanced back to see her. Slowly the nurses moved out. Suddenly I felt someone call my name. It was a nurse who informed me that the doctor wanted to see me.

When I walked towards his cabin, I was afraid of what he would say.

Oh God, let him say, that she is fine. She would breathe again. She will live with me. She will smile again at me. Please God! I will love her forever! I made promises to Him all the time while I walked towards the doctor's cabin.

"She is in a really bad state," he said.

It is so easy for these men in white to say those words, words which can break or shatter one completely.

"What is the problem doctor?" I asked him, gathering all my courage.

"She has been hit badly. Her spine has been the one to take the maximum impact. We are trying our best to save her life, but I am doubtful."

"Doubtful? About?" I asked waiting for the next bomb he would drop on me.

"I have doubts, that she may never be able to walk again," the doctor told in a soft voice as though he hadn't said it and I had imagined it all.

"She won't be able to walk? Is that it?" That seemed to be nothing compared to losing her completely.

"Son, it is easy for you to say. It'll be the hardest thing for her."

"You needn't worry about that doctor. Just save her life. She means the world to me. I need her to live. I want to see her alive. Please save her." I pleaded with moist eyes.

"We shall do our best," he said. I slowly rose and left the place.

Her family was as badly shaken as I was. They all tried to comfort me while I was busy doing the same for them. Her parents were the most distraught. Yet they seemed to be strong for my sake. Those days made us bond more than we ever had.

Diane was unconscious for the next three days. Three days which were the hardest for us. Our friends and family, all were worried. Everyone visited us. For me, to see her breathe was such a relief. Whenever I saw her, the only thing which was on my mind was to see her body rise and fall, which indicated that she was breathing. Breathing, alive, staying in my life.

The day came when she woke from her deep slumber. The day she opened her eyes, gave me hope to live again. It was like her eyes sunned my life, they washed away the pains and worries about losing her. Those brown eyes, on her pale and bruised face; the tiredness in them, made me wish if I could take away her pain. If I could share her pain and fill her life with all the happiness.

I thought it was all going to be good again, as it had been earlier. I wasn't prepared for what was to come after.

It was like there was no life left in Diane. When she opened her eyes and saw me and her family around, her tired face and pale eyes looked around hazily yet there was a peace. Slowly when she started to move her limbs around, she glanced at me and her mother. We both knew that the question could not be eluded. Before we could prepare ourselves, she spoke, "Mom? Chris? Can you please call the doctor? I think something is not right."

I walked up to her side and kissed softly on her forehead. She smiled back, "I know you were worried a lot Chris. I am so sorry for causing all this worry to all of you."

Then she asked me to bend my head, and whispered softly to me, "Call the doc Chris. Have they bandaged me too tight or have they given some medicine to me?"

I knew what she was talking about and there was no use beating around the bush. Her mother suddenly got up. With tears she said, "C'mon everyone. Let us leave these two alone for some time."

She looked up at me. I knew she wanted me to tell it to her. It wasn't something she could tell to her own daughter when she herself was unable to cope with it.

She'd held me and cried when I had told her about Diane's accident and her critical condition. When I had told her about the doctor's fears, she broke a little more. It was as if, a stone was thrown at a glass window and its pieces kept falling one by one. Every time she saw me, those wrinkled, beautiful and caring eyes got filled with tears.

I swallowed when they all left us alone. I pulled the small chair and sat on it. I was scared of her reaction but we had to tell her sooner or later. As far as I knew Diane, it had to be sooner.

"Di, listen sweetheart," I began.

"Chris! For God's sake why don't you just call in the doctor? Let me tell him about this strange thing I am feeling. Rather not feeling," she hissed angrily.

"What is it you want to know, love?"

"I cannot move my feet, not a single movement by my toes or knee or my leg. Rather I feel like, I can see my lower body but I don't feel like I have one. Now will you please call the doctor? I need to tell them about it, right?"

"They told us that already." I couldn't tell her more softly than this. I slowly stroked her hand

"What do you mean?" she shouted at my face as she pulled her hand from me.

"Diane, we were extremely worried for your life. We are happy that you are alive and among us. Please don't worry and harm your progress. Now that you are out of danger, I am waiting to have you back!"

"What are you trying to tell me? You mean that I am back, alive and all, but I am not completely fine. You mean to say that from now on, I have to live without my legs?"

"Honey, please don't take it like that. You have no idea; how hellish these days have been for all of us. It is nothing. We all love you for who you are. I love you, Di!" My eyes were filled with tears when I said it, because I knew this was a big blow to her yet I felt it was not as much as her death would have been to me.

"Don't you talk nonsense to me Chris. Stop fooling around. Get out!" she suddenly shouted.

The nurses came running inside and asked me to leave. They gave her some injection, probably sedated her, for she needed to rest. I stood out looking at her fall asleep under the effect of the medicine. Knowing that she was asleep still made me nervy. I really hoped and prayed that she would be as strong as she always had been.

It was midnight when I was able to be beside her. I kept stroking her hair. I had checked my mails and had rescheduled some of the meetings. My business partner had been a great support. He let me be at the hospital without any worries. That is the benefit of having your closest friend as your business partner. They help you when you need it the most!

She slowly opened those mesmerizing eyes of hers and looked at me. Confused and heavy. Deep within them, I could see pain and sadness.

"Di, how are you?"

"Mmmm. I am better now. What time is it?"

"It is midnight dear."

"Are you not going to go home?"

"Not until you return."

"You should rest Chris. I am fine now. Go get some sleep."

"Don't worry about me. I become fine only when I see you. I will be fine as long as you are with me."

"Go home Chris. Please. Take rest. I insist."

"No. Please don't ask me to go. Anyway I will be going in the morning as I have to attend some meetings. It's urgent else I wouldn't have gone."

"You haven't been to office since the day I came here, isn't it?"

"You know me so perfectly well, darling," I said and kissed her forehead.

We kept talking until one of us fell asleep. I think it was me, as I didn't remember staring at her face while she slept. I was sure of that.

The next morning, I woke and left for my apartment. Diane hadn't woken up. I kissed her forehead and that little curve her lips made, was still embedded in my mind. I knew one thing for sure. Diane was mine. I couldn't live without her. This event had spread the roots deeper of the blooming tree of love.

I was unaware of the thoughts this incident left on Diane's mind. She started getting hypersensitive, moody and resentful. Nothing seemed to please her, however hard we tried. The day the nurse walked in her room with the wheelchair was the most horrifying for us. Diane just drove us away from the room threatening to shout and create a ruckus in the whole place. As hours passed she realized that she had no other way out. The tempest in her started to recede; at least that's what she showed us. Things were gnawing her from within. I could feel it.

In another week, she was discharged from the hospital. Her mother was nervous and worried if she would be able to take care of 'this' Diane. Nothing is as saddening as the helplessness of a caring mother. I promised to help her and Diane in everything that lay ahead of us.

I went over every day after work. My dinners were always with Diane and her family. Day by day she started getting annoyed at me. She started getting pessimistic. I knew where it came from. Her outlook towards life had changed, and so did it change for our love and me. I was not prepared to let her drive me away. There was no way she could do that to me. I knew I loved her, I knew she loved me, and I knew I wanted to spend the rest of my life with her.

A week before our marriage, while we were out to have our meeting with the wedding planner, Diane was driving her mad. The wedding planner finally left without coming to any conclusion but with a lot of uncertainty looming in her mind. I could feel what was coming.

"Chris."

"Mmmmm," I murmured sipping my coffee at the coffee shop where we had just had our disastrous meeting with the planner.

"I am serious now and I want you to listen seriously."

"When are you not serious, Di?" I smirked.

"Listen to me. I have thought long about this," she paused for a while and then continued, "I want to call off this marriage."

The sky seemed to move closer to hit me on the head. I thought she was being childish and stupid, but I knew that this woman had lost her mind.

"What nonsense, Di!"

"I am serious about it."

"No way. Why do you want to do that?"

Her eyes welled up as she looked at me, "Can't you see? I had an accident, but it seems like you have lost your eyesight! You can't marry me. You don't want to!"

I was angered. What did she know? How did she know, what I wanted? Who was she to tell me what I wanted?

"Diane! Listen for once and carefully. I am not going to call off the marriage. I am marrying you on the day and date we had fixed up. You do not have any idea what I want."

"Why do you want to marry me? You want to marry me, though I am nothing but a crippled woman, really? Marry me, who won't be able to live a normal life, someone who won't give you a normal home? I don't want your pity and mercy, Chris."

I got up from my seat and walked closer to her. She sat cold and stiff on her wheelchair. I bent down in front of her and held her hands in mine. She pulled them away. Her coldness was killing me. I knew anything I told her now would be of no use.

I walked out of the coffee shop. A few moments out in the air would perhaps give me something to tell her and convince her about my love. The cool breeze out reminded me how Diane loved walking in it. How she would sway and sing, cuddle and snuggle up to me! How she would give me those teasing glances and kisses! If only she knew what pain it was when I had had to live those moments, when I was afraid that she wouldn't make it out alive from the clutches of death.

I stood a few steps away, leaning on a lamp post, tired and helpless!

Suddenly, I saw a pretty woman, maybe in her early twenties, flying and galloping with the wind, holding onto a single balloon walking towards the coffee shop. My Diane was so much like her. All lively and joyful. Tears filled my eyes thinking of her.

I walked slowly on the pavement. I saw the helpless eyes of that man outside, leaning on the lamp post. They showed how exhausted and tired he was. Instantly I knew she was around. There was gloominess around the yellow aura of love. He loved her. He loved her enough to feel the pain that she was enduring.

He loved her enough to understand her unspoken words. While, she was trying to move him away, thinking that it would help him. It wasn't that she had doubts about his love, but she knew there was no other way to drive him away from her. I knew all of it, so I had to do what I had come here for.

I walked into the café and sat on the chair opposite her and looked at her. She raised her eyes to me. I smiled and so did she.

"Hey!" I said.

"Hello!" she replied calmly. Her eyes kept searching for him.

"You drive him away and then wait anxiously for him," I said teasingly to break the silence that prevailed between us.

"Excuse me?" she seemed confused.

"Don't do this to him."

"What are you talking about? Who are you?"

"I'm just a friend, someone who wants to help you."

"I need no help," her words were firm but her voice was unsteady. She was trying to be strong but deep within she was crumbling.

"Yes my dear. You need no help. Do you know something? You are blessed. You are blessed with the treasure of love. You are throwing it away or rather discarding it away. Don't do that! Only a few lucky ones are given such a beautiful love. Don't reject or refuse it."

"Who are you? What do you know? What a terrible feeling it is to live like this; to see the man you love, ready to marry you, even though you are crippled, to see him stand there doing everything for you while you are unable to do a single thing for him, to see him spoil his life because he loves you."

"What makes you think he won't be happy if he marries you? What makes you feel that he wants you to do anything for him! What makes you think that he is spoiling his life by marrying you? Stop making your own assumptions. People end up taking the most erroneous decisions because they assume. Do you not see the love in his eyes and heart? Can you not feel his pain when you do this to him and yourself? This won't drive him away. This will destroy him. He died every moment of that time when you were unconscious. His eyes were fixed at your body, striving to see your chest rise and fall to be assured that you were breathing. No one deserves to be paid back like this for loving you."

She was confused and amazed that I knew everything. I slowly felt her thoughts rushing and racing within her mind. Now I knew what could make her stop her tirade. Leaving her lost in her own thoughts, I slowly moved away and stepped out of the café.

He was still standing there. Alone and feeling lost. I started walking towards him.

The girl with the single balloon walked out of the coffee shop and started coming in my direction. She held it so tight as though her life depended on it. She kept getting closer and something in me told that she was here for me. She came to help. What help? Where and how?

She stood in front of me and smiled. Her angelic face and her innocent smile, made me smile back.

"Go. Tell her. Tell her all."

I stood in utter surprise. What was she talking about?

"Go inside and tell her. Tell her everything. Don't let your love down or let her craziness change your decision. Live and fight for your love when needed."

Saying this to me, she walked away. I was fixed to the ground and it took a few moments to realize what she had said. With a new energy and passion, I rushed back into the coffee shop and saw her sitting there silently. She looked to suffer as much pain as I was enduring. I knew only one thing and it was that I loved her. I loved her more than I could ever love. I wasn't ready to let her drive me away.

I walked up to her; she raised her eyes to see me. I saw them moist and filled with love for me. I bent down in front of her, I was on my knees.

I held her hands in mine and said, "Diane. I've wanted to marry you ever since my heart told me about its feelings for you. I have always wanted to have you as mine in front of this world. I love you and your happiness means the world to me. I am marrying you because I love you. And love cannot be on par with pity. Please don't do this. I won't let you do it. I want to live the rest of my life with you, the very thought of being away from you kills me. Don't shove me away, my love."

Diane's tears now fell uncontrollably. She lifted my hand to her lips and kissed the back of it. I gripped her hand tighter within mine and kissed her hand. I raised my upper body and placed my lips on her forehead and kissed her long softly. My tears fell on her face and her tears fell on my hand. As I embraced her, the other people in the cafe who were watching us started applauding.

Just then I turned towards the window. There she was holding on to that single balloon, with a few words on it. Diane looked at the same spot and smiled. Then it struck me.

The Girl.

The Balloon.

The Balloon Girl had come for us. She smiled at us, and the balloon rose up in the air. It had words, four words for us!

STAY IN LOVE!

ALWAYS!

Don't Stop Dreaming

Standing near the bridge, I saw the water gush below. There was serenity around, but all the people who walked were so engrossed in their mobile screens that they didn't lift their eyes and watch the white clouds hovering in the sky and the blue water below. They were unconcerned about the cool breeze around. I sat on the bench, waiting. I knew very soon, that person would be here too.

Tara looked at herself in the mirror. In her plain, light blue tunic and black jeans, she looked like any other plain Jane. Her hair was tied up in a ponytail. She put on some kohl and smiled at herself. Maybe that was the last time she would see herself in that mirror. She sneaked out of the room as she quietly pulled out her white crochet overcoat. It was gifted to her by her grandmother after she passed her tenth class exams. It was going to be with her today.

She had topped in the school that time. It was nearly two years ago. Now grandma wasn't there to help her, to understand and save her. The day grandma breathed her last a year ago, Tara had felt lonelier than any of the children of the woman. She had lost her pillar, her strength and the woman who always told her, 'When you dream for something, let not any hurdle stop you from attaining it!' She was the only one who knew what Tara loved the most, what she always wanted to become.

As Tara walked out, she watched Mother busy in the kitchen. She stood for some time, trying to absorb the movements of her mother before she would close her eyes. Sadly, Dad had gone to work. She saw his photograph hanging in her room. He was her best friend, her strong supporter and her critic. She loved him more than anything. She was the one who had given him nothing to be proud of. She had disappointed him. She always wanted to stay his favourite child and his pride, but ever since the results, she knew she had failed him.

With a deep breath she waited. She was waiting for the right chance and she was gifted one by Lady Luck. It did surprise her that she showed some compassion now. Not when she had done so much hard work and was hoping that destiny would be kind to her.

She walked unhesitatingly. She knew where she was going. She didn't even need any money. She had a letter in the pocket of her blue jacket which she wore over her black jeans and blue top. She had carried her shoes, so that she could tip toe out of the house and then wear them for her final walk in these lanes. She was finally able to sneak out of her house.

Walking for about ten minutes, she proceeded towards her destination. She always loved coming there. Dad and Mom always held her hand as they walked with her, admiring the beauty of the sky. They were perfect parents, but she hadn't been a perfect child for them. This guilt was eating away her soul. Finally, she reached the place. She stood by the far end of the bridge and saw others walk by.

As she kept observing all around, she saw a little girl with her parents. The pink frock complemented her skin tone, and her little ponytails swayed as she moved her head. She was cheerfully laughing away as she jumped in the air clinging onto their hands. Tara had so many memories of the days she had held her dad's fingers and walked on that stony bridge. She remembered the times, when she was young and Dad would lift her up and carry her on his shoulder. She remembered how she would team up with Mom while eating the ice cream and laugh away when Dad's ice cream would either melt away or slip from his hands. There were innumerable memories, uncountable moments when they had loved her more than anything.

Yet, she had broken all the trust and shaken the pride they had in her. They always boasted about her good grades and percentage in front of their friends, colleagues and relatives. She couldn't have just shattered it for them. She had become nothing but a liability for them, though they had always regarded her as an asset.

She sat on one of the wooden benches fixed there to rest and observed the beauty of the river underneath and the limitless sky above. She had some time more, she felt. She sat reminiscing the days she had spent at home, the days she had lived on this planet, in that loving house with those beautiful people.

She still remembered when her aunt had suddenly visited their house. Dad was glad to see her come. His sister always had a special place in his heart. He got annoyed when she advised him to stop Tara's education and get her married. This sudden concern from her aunt was gurgling since one of her elder cousin's wedding had been fixed. Just because she was the next female in the progeny, their relatives wanted to see her "settled".

'Education and career were issues of the boys. Girls shouldn't be entrusted with these things,' she had said. She was even offering to look for good proposals for Tara.

All this for a seventeen-year-old girl, who was just going to appear for her class twelve examinations in three months.

On top of that she was insensitive enough to discuss and berate the whole female species, in front of the innocent and confused girl. After that event, Tara always wondered how she could be so harsh towards the gender. Wasn't she a member of the same too?

When Mom saw the discussion becoming awkward for Tara, she pulled her out of the room and asked her to get back to her project work. She helped her daughter through it. The mother couldn't sit there quiet while the brother and sister spoke about it. Surprisingly no one asked her about it, though she was the one who had brought the child into this world.

Tara knew her mom's stance was clear and so was Dad's. Such conservative thoughts of the society wouldn't bog them down.

They were educated people and wanted Tara to pursue her dream.

Dad and Mom, both were doctors. So she had inherited the dream of becoming a doctor too. It wasn't really her dream. She was never in a position to dream. Her parents' success and profession was in a subtle way thrust on her and as a way to show her love and appreciation, she was more than willing to do it; just to make them proud of her.

Today she was so heavily burdened by guilt for she had broken all their dreams and ashamed them.

She had been a good student all along. Her grades were worth boasting and her parents always took pride in her achievements. The only thing they didn't approve of was her hobby - painting. They felt she was spending time in unwanted things. They always advised her to use it to study. While for her, painting wasn't just a hobby. It had a soothing effect on her which she couldn't explain to anyone. Her brushes, her colors, the palette and the blank canvas called her to unleash the thoughts in her mind and heart.

A few days ago, Mom had scolded her for spending too much time and asked her to end this foolishness, for there were bigger goals they had in mind for her, higher levels to achieve and more important work than splashing colors on a white, colourless sheet. Angrily Mom had packed off all her things into a carton and shifted it to the store room. No one was allowed to bring out things from there unless Mom allowed. They never knew what it meant to her.

She felt dejected and the final blow came last Sunday, when she was waiting for the result of the entrance test to get the medical seat. She had worked extremely hard and was hopeful of doing well. Destiny had something else in mind.

She failed to get a good rank. On the contrary she had failed to even get the minimum score in the entrance examination.

She was shocked and her parents were upset and displeased. They felt their dreams had come to naught. When she spoke to her Art's teacher, the only person who appreciated her talent, she felt a little peaceful. Shraddha Ma'am had been her class teacher and was concerned, so she came home the next day. She tried to convince Mom that Tara was a good student and a talented artist. She wanted Tara to join a Painting workshop to learn more. It filled Tara's heart with boundless joy to hear about it.

In an instant Mom turned cold towards the guest. She told in a very firm voice, "Ma'am, I respect you as Tara's teacher and am glad you care for her. She is my daughter and I know what's best for her. I will not let my daughter sit and waste her life, playing with colours. We are a family of doctors and we cannot let some Arts teacher come and influence her. I can see that it is your influence that had distracted her from her goals. If only you hadn't been filling her mind with such ridiculous ideas, she would have been more focused on her aim and got a good rank. For her failure to get a good rank, I hold you responsible."

Tara was dumbstruck. She had never seen Mom talk like that with anyone. Why was she behaving like that with her favourite teacher? Why was her failure being put on her teacher?

"But Mom, it is my fault. Shraddha Ma'am always encouraged me in everything. Please don't talk to her like that," Tara whispered to her mother when she came into the kitchen to take the tray of tea.

"Tara, you stay out of this. That woman has made a mess of her life and now she plans to do the same for you. I am your mother. Don't I know what's good for you? She will never intrude in my child's life anymore now."

Tara was confused. Her eyes were filled with tears. 'Why was Shraddha Ma'am being targeted? Was it because she uncovered the hidden talent with me? Was it because she taught me that it's important in life to do what you love? Was it because she allowed me to spill out my feelings with the strokes of brushes?'

With such thoughts whirling in her mind, she saw Shraddha Ma'am quietly sip her tea. A few minutes later, she got up to leave. She just cast a glance at Tara who stood hiding behind the kitchen door. Tara was sad that her mother had spoken so rudely to her teacher and didn't want to come out in front of her, but her teacher's face had a simple smile. A smile which convinced Tara that her teacher didn't regret anything she had taught Tara. Nor did she hold Tara responsible for the way her mother had behaved.

The guilt of breaking the trust and heart of the people most important to her was too huge a burden for Tara to carry. She felt helpless. Anything she did - after the results were declared - was regarded wrong. Everything she said was misinterpreted, anything she did was declared erratic or faulty. She had never thought that by not clearing the entrance test she had committed such a grave sin that her mother wouldn't talk to her anymore in her usual way. Neither would Dad spend time with her, like he used to do earlier. Her little brother and sister, Rahul and Priya, were unaware of the reason but they knew that their beloved sister had done something, very wrong! They tried to cheer her up, but all in vain.

Today, exactly a week later, all her courage and hopes had flickered and died slowly like a waning candle. In a week's time, the courageous Tara had been replaced by a weak one. Last night her weakness had made her take one decision; which might just be her last decision.

Sitting alone on the weak wooden bench, she watched the waves rise and fall. People said life was also like that, it pushes you up, makes you rise but also brings you down, pulls you to fall. People forget to say that when you rise everyone is there with you; while when you fall you are left alone. You have to either fight to rise back or let the waves drown you down mercilessly. Tara was here for the latter.

Slowly she took a deep breath and walked closer towards the parapet of the bridge. She placed her burning hands on the cold metal of the structure and tightened her grip on it. She had to do it. She had to do it fast. Fast enough, so that no one could stop her.

Her brown eyes were set on the horizon while the wind blew her hair across her face. She let the soothing air pass through every pore of her body. A body that felt like a coffin as it tried to contain her troubled soul. She loosened the grip on the railing, after deciding her plan of action. Instantly she felt a warm hand on hers. She looked down and saw a young lady's soft hand covering her little one. She turned to look at the person to whom it belonged. She had been right. It was a young woman, probably in her twenties.

"Hey young lady! What a beautiful spot to watch the horizon and the waves!" she remarked.

Tara was surprised, all along the sidewalk there were many people. Leaving all of them, this woman had to come forward to talk to her. She was surprised and felt a tinge of regret that she couldn't carry out her plan now.

"Yes Ma'am," she softly replied.

"Is everything alright?" she asked with concern. "You seem to be quite low in spirit."

Tara was surprised that a stranger should suddenly come and ask about her spirit and feelings.

"Yes Ma'am, everything is alright. I am feeling quite well," she lied.

"Sometimes it helps when you share with someone the demons you are fighting with," she said as Tara tried to pull out the hand from her grip.

Tara raised her head and looked into the eyes of the young woman. She was nearly the same age of Shraddha Ma'am and the same concern and warmth was there in her eyes. Tara felt a connection with this beautiful stranger. What could it be? Why was her heart bursting with emotions? She was afraid that one more time she questioned her, all the feelings suppressed down would erupt. Why did this stranger seem like an old friend, a well-wisher, and a helper?

"Tell me dear," she said in a whisper as she firmly held Tara's hands in hers. That was enough to bring out the storm that lay within Tara's heart for nearly a week. Tara looked into those blue eyes and her brown eyes started flowing with tears.

The young woman pulled her away from the parapet and holding her hand took her to the bench where Tara had been sitting since she had reached the bridge. She let Tara cry, alternatively rubbing her hands and her back. So much warmth was exuded by her that Tara just let the tears flow. Words didn't come. She just cried her heart out. Slowly her crying slowed down.

The young woman opened the bag that was on her shoulder and took out a small water bottle. Handing it to Tara she said, "Have some water Tara." As Tara gulped down a little water, she felt calmness within her. She then started telling everything. She told the woman about how she had failed in fulfilling the dreams of her parents.

The woman quietly heard it all. She passed no judgement. She said nothing but kept listening. When Tara had said it all, she felt like a weakling, a wounded bird which had wings but couldn't fly. Except the plan of action that brought her here to the bridge, she told the woman everything. Tara was shocked when the woman spoke as she seemed to know that already!

"Life is too beautiful Tara. It is too beautiful to be sacrificed for a little fall or failure. Life isn't just the celebrations, it is also the battles lost, dreams shattered. If everyone started thinking like you, then what would life mean? You do not decide when, where and how you will come into this world. Then how can you take the decision to take away something that isn't even yours? How can you destroy something that the Creator has entrusted you with? When you didn't decide when you'll cry for the first time in this world, how can you decide when will be your last?

A closed door doesn't mean the end of the world; it means that the door is just not right for you. Maybe your door is somewhere else waiting for you to come and unlock it. Failing in an examination isn't worth to put your life to end."

Tara realized how true her words were. Her crying had resulted in hiccups and she drank more water to stop them.

"Tara, for once did you think, how would your parents feel? How can you punish them? Your weakness and failure is your problem. You can't let your problem destroy them. Your irrational decision today could bring in disastrous consequences. They would hold themselves responsible for this and that guilt would work like poison for them. Think about that!"

At that time Tara thought about the affects her decision would have on her parents and siblings. She was proving to the world that she was a weak person.

"What do I do? My life feels like a burden. I feel like I am not the able daughter of my parents. Rather I am a darkness that has engulfed everyone who is around me. What else can I do?"

She waited for the woman to answer her and guide her in making the right decision.

"Why do you think that way? Rather if you do what was in your mind, you will be responsible for the unending pain and trauma your parents will face. Why don't you get back to what your heart tells you to do? Why don't you get back to the hobby of yours? Nowadays even that, the art, has emerged as a strong career option. Don't worry if they stop you now, for soon enough, they will know your pain and realize that nothing is more important than inner peace."

"No! They won't ever understand. They will never allow me. No one sees that as a success." Tara cried in sorrow.

"In that case, come with me. I will show you something." The stranger pulled Tara up and got her steady on her feet.

"Come? Where should I go with you? Mom said I shouldn't talk to or go with strangers."

A smile spread around the stranger's face. "Don't worry we aren't going anywhere. You see that gallery hall there," she said pointing towards the structure at the end of the bridge. It was hardly twenty steps away from where Tara stood. It was a public place and her fear receded.

"We are going there," the stranger said with a firm voice.

Tara nodded her head and walked alongside her. She was afraid if the woman would harm her, but her heart said she was just being hysterical. As Tara reached there, she was in for a big surprise.

There was a big poster, announcing the event of the day at the gallery. It was a painting exhibition of a very renowned artist, Uma Bansal. As Tara walked along the corridor, she was amazed to see the paintings hanging by the walls. The colours were emotions on canvas. The lines showed the grace and beauty of everything they were depicting. Each painting spoke a different story.

A teary-eyed little boy.

A veiled young woman struggling to carry earthen pots on her head.

The vacant desert with an illusion of the oasis.

All of them had their own tale. All seemed to be telling their accounts to Tara.

Suddenly, she felt a tap on her shoulder.

"Hello young lady!" Hearing the voice, Tara turned and saw an older woman, in a simple light blue cotton saree. It had little embroidered white flowers at the borders. Her fine wrinkles and the sparkle in her eyes added an elegance and beauty to her face.

She was old and she had the warmth that reminded her of her grandmother. Tara felt she had found a kindred spirit.

"Hello Ma'am! I was just...just..." She started looking around for the young woman who brought her there. She wasn't present there.

"I know you were just looking at the paintings. I was amused by the time you were spending at each painting. What are you seeing so closely?"

"Oh! I didn't know we had to see them quickly and move out," Tara innocently replied.

The old woman laughed at Tara's confusion. "No dear girl. I have seen people walk past a painting after a single glance. I was wondering what made you stand and observe them so closely. I wanted to know what you found so interesting in my paintings."

Tara was awestruck when she was able to gradually place that smiling face. She was the famous artist herself. Tara had always dreamt of meeting artists and Uma Bansal topped the list. Today it came true. The day couldn't have been better.

"Oh my God!" Tara could only utter those words as she cupped her face and her eyes widened.

The woman smiled warmly and put her soft hands on Tara's head. She stroked it gently and asked, "Tell me dear, what made you stand there, observing them so intently?"

"I didn't realize that I was really observing them long enough, to be noticed by you. I was just watching them and felt like each one was speaking to me, telling me the stories they had within them. I was just unaware of the things around me. They meant everything to me at that time, at that moment. That's it."

"That's really wonderful! I am happy to see someone like you, a person of today's unstoppable generation being so interested in art and paintings like that. This shows that there is hope in the future for this art too, in the rat race of survival." She smiled with sadness.

Tara was confused. "Why do you think like that, Ma'am?" she blurted out. Uma Bansal put her shoulder around Tara and they started walking. She started telling the little girl about herself.

"I know how the world is competitive out there. I know the battle for survival when you step out into the world. If everyone is going to jump into the rat race then, who will carry forward the legacy and tradition of these amazing arts? These arts seem to be slowly dying with the advancements in technology and the mistaken beliefs. Indeed, it is difficult to make a mark soon in this field. You may not earn from day one. I ask, is inner peace and satisfaction nothing? When I started as an artist, a painter to be precise, I knew I wouldn't be able to earn a day's meal with it."

"I had to manage a day job and squiggle out time for my hobby. Life brought in new priorities and new responsibilities. People thought I was mad, but I managed to keep my dreams alive. People around me were out to dampen that burning flame within me. I strived hard. Slowly I was managing both sides. The practical survival was with the money I earned money for survival from the job and my soul's peace by the passion I had within me. Things today have turned into a state where I am seen as a famous painter. No one knows the struggle I had gone through to reach here."

She stopped talking and their walk came to an end. Hanging before her was a big life size painting. Undoubtedly it was a beautiful painting of sunrise. The painting gave her a sense of déjà vu.

There was a girl standing on the bridge, watching the water flowing under it. Her hair was blown onto her face. The sun was high up in the horizon and the darkness still lurking around. The artist had shown in her unique way how the light of the sun was slowly driving away the darkness. The girl was watching the sun glowing. In her right hand she was holding a bag, out of which peeped a few brushes and a few rolled up sheets.

In that instant, seeing that painting Tara knew what life had in store for her. She would fight back. She would be a warrior, not a weakling. She was ready to take up the challenges life was going to throw at her. She knew it would need a lot of courage and patience but she would do it. She had to do it. She wasn't going to waste the precious gift of life.

Engrossed in seeing her reflection in the painting, she knew what she was going to do. She turned to thank Uma for her words. Unknowingly the old woman had given her new life, new hope. She thanked her profusely. Tara was surprised when she said, "You don't need to thank me. Thank her, who brought you here!"

Then it struck her, where had that young woman gone. She looked around in the gallery. She was nowhere to be seen. She quickly stepped out and walked again towards the bridge where she had met that unknown friend. There she stood, just as Tara had stood before meeting her. Now she was holding a bunch of colorful balloons in her hand. They were vibrant, coloured ones, waiting to fly into the sky.

She ran up to her and put her hands around the waist of her 'new' friend. She stood behind her and hugged her.

"Thank you!" she said aloud, "Thank you for helping me."

The friend turned around and bent down, "Don't thank me for anything Tara. Just remember that life is to be valued, to be cherished, to be lived. You cannot just let little falls become the end of it. Remember, when need arises, someday, become the hand that comes to hold another from falling. Be sensitive to those around you. You never know who might just need that little smile, those little words of hope and motivation. Try to be that flower whose beauty and fragrance gives an onlooker or a passerby a reason to smile. Don't forget yourself in this crowd.

Don't let the world bring another Tara to the verge of the bridge as it had done today."

Tara nodded her head affirmatively and promised, "Yes! I promise to do it. I will try to be for others, what you have been for me today."

She handed over all the balloons to Tara and said, "Let go of all your fears and sadness, Tara. Let go of all those things that pull you down. Watch them fly away from you and feel that peace and calmness. See them leave you and reach the sky. See them go away from your view. Don't let the world's chaos drown the bubbling passions of yours. Smile and spread more smiles Tara. Always."

Tara smiled and as gestured by her friend, she let the balloons leave her grip one by one. As the balloons rose up she felt a strange peace in her. A soothing calmness filled her as her eyes watched the colourful balloons fill up the sky. She heard soft claps and turned to see a little girl clapping with a sweet smile spread on her face. A little ahead was a young boy, with tears streaming his face, but smiling innocently. She realized how wonderful it felt to spread smiles, even if they were strangers for you. She turned to tell her friend about her new found peace and happiness, but she was not there.

She had gone away as quietly as she had walked into Tara's life. Suddenly realization struck her. She had read a few stories on a blog she followed, about a young woman who walked in and helped people in distress. That was in faraway places. Was it really her? Did she really come here, to help Tara in her trouble?

Was she the one, whom they called…. **The balloon girl?**

Let Happiness In

Strolling along the beach, there was a quirky uneasiness in my heart. Something tugged my heart. It was a familiar feeling I got when I was supposed to move ahead to the next person who needed me. Today I wasn't able to know where I had to be. Somehow this place seemed the right place to be, yet I felt out of place. What was it I had to do here? Who was it I had to meet here? I passed my eyes across the beach and just then I knew which spot I had to walk to.

There is no pain, no ache as great as laying someone whom you loved, to eternal sleep. There is nothing that can hurt a mother's heart more than seeing your child close her eyes lying in your lap. There is nothing as difficult as watching the breathing slow down and then end in a whimper. The most difficult is to see the body get pale and be dressed up for the last rituals.

It is heart wrenching to see these things when your mind is flooded with memories of the child as she ran around you with little complaints and problems. The times you peeped into the room while the little one wriggled and mumbled even in sleep make you smile even with tears flowing. The moments you heard her hum songs and stomp her feet while her mood fluctuated bring a grin on your sad face. The days when you've seen her fall in love and get married make your heart heavy with emotions. Suddenly all those memories play back in your mind, while before your eyes she lies still, unmoving. Dead as a rock, silent in the coffin.

"It is a hard time for you, Martha."

"May the Lord bless her soul."

"She was a beautiful girl, gone too soon."

"She is in a better place."

Friends and relatives who had come for the funeral of Janice spoke words of consolation. All spoke with grief and sorrow but their words didn't console me. They seemed like just words handed over as a polite way of meeting and greeting me. No one was telling me how wrong it was that the Creator had just taken away the love of my life. The worst was to hear - "You need to be brave now, otherwise who will take care of the little one."

I dreaded hearing this, I hated knowing this and nothing in my heart was there for the little one. She was the one responsible for the pain I had to endure from today till I died.

Janice was just twenty-two. She had been the only daughter I had after two sons. She was the lifeline of the house. Chirpy and naughty, she was adored by her brothers for her witty words and problem solving ideas. She was the little princess of her father. The first day she went to school, her first nursery rhyme, her scribbling on the papers in her books and then on the wall, all these were memories embedded in our minds.

Her sleepover parties, her first crush on the neighbour's son, her first heartbreak when she came to know he was already dating someone else were the little experiences of life she had learnt. Her wish to join college and dream to become a fashion magazine editor were the goals she had set for herself and would keep talking continuously about them. In her short lifespan she had managed to do so many things and left us with a treasure of memories.

As a mother, it broke me down. I knew it hurt him more than me, I knew it for sure. Still he stood there as strong as a mountain, collecting the memories of hers even here. Jason, I knew was in more agony than I.

"Keep smiling Mom," her words echoed in my mind, "You never know what the other person might be going through. Your smile might just change the way he sees things. Remember it burns more calories." She would giggle and walk out of the door of the kitchen.

Tears sprung to my eyes as I thought that she would never walk in again into that kitchen. There would be no more giggles from her. She would not throw tantrums while getting ready for a party. No more memories that would be created with us. The girl had left us with just a little more than twenty years of hers to be treasured by us, as long as we lived.

As her friends and colleagues spoke about how wonderful she was as a person, I kept recollecting how easily she would mingle with people and make friends. She infected everyone with her sweet smile. I was lost in my thoughts until Edward stood up. The man I had begun to hate. He had first taken her away from us. Now he stood there beside his mother telling the world how he had lost someone so special in his life. I never knew that the man whom Janice loved would be the man I would dread the rest of my life. Suddenly, the bundle wrapped in a white cloth held by his mother gave a cry. It pierced my ears and my heart. I felt its pain but I couldn't bring myself to feel anything for it. I just knew I hated the father and the daughter.

After the coffin was lowered and the events came to an end the guests started walking away. Only six of us were left - her brothers Ewan and Matt, her parents - Jason and I, and the two who were related to my girl. It was now that the boys lost control of their tears and landed with their knees on the soft brown mud that covered the grave.

Both of them had been silent since the doctors had declared her 'brought in dead'. They had just been silently making arrangements. They had been seated at the table, listening to the arrangements being made and giving inputs where needed. They had been doing their duties mechanically. Now after their little sister was set in her little coffin that lay deep down in the grave, with flowers covering it and spreading a soft fragrance, their patience had run out.

As a mother, it was a woeful scene. Two grown up men, sobbing like little boys, touching and rubbing the mud, as though caressing their beloved sister. Jason walked closer and stood between them. He bent and kept his hands on their shoulders, trying to console them. Instantly, he sat down and ran his arms across their shoulders. They both hugged him and cried. Standing a few steps behind them, I knew how hard it had been for them.

A similar scene was a few steps away, with Edward sitting near the grave and talking to the woman whose hand he had come and asked from us. My heart told me he was as shattered as we were but somehow I wasn't able to make myself go to him and console him. Jason walked towards him while I moved towards my sons. They needed me more.

I walked carrying a bottle of water and few paper cups that were left unused. They looked up at me while I handed them water one by one. My tears had to wait. I couldn't just break down here. It would make it more difficult for the men in the family to see me break now. The mother's instinct advised me to be the strong pillar for my family, for if all the pillars shake, the building could collapse. That was not what Janice or I would want or allow to happen.

Slowly they got up and I held their hands as I walked between them. Jason was still with Edward. He was holding that bundle in his hands. The old wrinkled face of Jason had a little smile as he kept staring at the face. We walked closer and I could see the tiny head and the features. She was just like Janice had been when she was born. Tiny fingers with sharp pink nails made up the little hand. Her thin pink lips were curved in a smile. A smile that was so similar to Janice's. Her golden curls barely covered the head. For a moment I felt I was seeing Janice again as a baby in Jason's arms.

"Mom! Isn't she beautiful?" Ewan's voice brought me back into the reality.

I looked at Ewan and tears filled my eyes. A lump rose in my throat and I just walked away from there. I didn't even once turn or see when they started moving away from Edward. It was then that tears started flowing down my eyes. I couldn't stop them. I couldn't even feel them fall on my cheek. They just streamed down my face, as my patience had ended for the day. I walked up to the car and just waited for them. When I heard their footsteps close by, I wiped my tears away with the back of my hands.

"Here, take this." A handkerchief came up in my blurry vision and I saw Jason passing on his white handkerchief to me. I took it and wiped off my tears, unable to utter a word or even blink an eye without another tear falling from it.

Just like the drive to the church for the funeral, the same silence prevailed when we drove back home. We were returning home leaving Janice all alone. My daughter had always been the centre of attraction with her wit and her intelligence, but today she was all alone. No one would be there with her. All her life she had people around her who loved her but now she lay there.

At dinner we all sat across the dining table but we hardly spoke. Each one of us had tears in our eyes as we tried to push food down our throats. No one took her name, no one spoke a word, no one reminded or recollected any incident of hers, but all of us were walking down the lanes of our memories filled with moments with her. Her chirpy voice, her impatience, her laughter at the stupidest joke of her father, everything just created a chaos in that silent hall.

People say it is difficult when someone leaves. Undoubtedly it is, and it is most difficult to see the impact of their departure on the people around. Like a soulless body, the house was void of any sound, any sign of life.

Clearing the tables, discarding the untouched food from the plates and keeping the left over in the refrigerator, I tried to keep myself engrossed in work. I didn't know what would happen when I would walk towards our room. Her room was just across ours. It had been till she got married. I knew that walking in the hallway would kill me a thousand times all over again.

Ewan and Matt were twins and were born nearly five years after Janice. She had been there in our life after one year of our marriage. In simple words, she had been the one who was always a part of my life in this house. She was my daughter and my best friend. She was her father's princess and her brothers adored her for the love and the joy she spread around.

I still had the clear image in my memory of holding her just hours after she was born. Her first smile had filled me with a new happiness, for she had given me a new title, 'MOTHER'. Her tiny fingers as they encircled my finger, her soft pale skin and her little bud-like lips had made me fall in love with her all over again.

She was the best thing that God had given me. Why did He have to take her back so soon? She was so young. She had so many dreams, so many things in life she had aspired to do. There were so many plans she and Edward had made. There were so many wishes left unfulfilled, so many dreams shattered. As I wiped my hands on the apron after washing and re-washing the dishes, I felt a warm hand on my left shoulder.

"Martha, stop it," he said softly.

"Jason, I thought to clear up things before we sleep," I tried to give him a proper answer.

"That would have taken hardly fifteen minutes for you. It has been an hour."

Tears started rolling down my eyes. "I just can't Jason. I can't bear this pain. I can't walk up to our room and not peep into hers. Though I know now she will never sleep in that room. What do I do? I cannot sleep in that room there."

"How long will you avoid things Martha?" he asked as his voice shook. "How long will you avoid everything related to her? How many things will you avoid? Each thing in this house, around the house, on the roads we have travelled, all will remind you of her. How long will you hide from them? Can you remove them from your memories? Will this pain subside if you avoid these things?

Will your heartbreak be less if you get rid of the things that remind you of her?"

I nodded my head as words rose in my throat but ended up forming a lump. I just couldn't speak in so much pain.

"If that works for you, I would love to do so too. It won't. The more you avoid it, the more it will pain you."

It was then that I completely broke down. I cried and screamed. I shouted and complained against the Creator for taking away my little angel. I slumped on the cold kitchen floor and kept crying. Jason let go of his manly image and we both hugged each other and wept. We cried together like we always had laughed together.

When our breathing got slow and we were shuddering, we wiped each other's tears and sat there on the kitchen floor, leaning on to the door of the refrigerator, holding each other's hands firmly. Somehow, letting the storm within me spill out with Jason beside me had left me a little lighter. Neither had the pain left us nor would it ever lessen, but it felt like a burden was off our hearts. Trying to control your true emotions does that to us. We are so busy struggling to bind our emotions within that we don't realize how heavy it makes our soul.

Jason got up and filled a glass with water. He tried to make me drink. "Have at least a sip," he said and I couldn't tell him 'no'. I took the glass and drank the water, sip by sip. Jason smiled at me and I reciprocated. This man could just become the strongest support in times I fell short. Today seemed to be one day when I was falling short in every way and he was trying his best to help me out. He pulled me up and made me sit on the chair. He pulled out another one and sat in front of me, holding my hands in his.

"Martha, I know you have never really liked Edward. Do you really think it is his fault?"

"Of course. I have never liked that man and now I will never be able to forgive him for this. He and that daughter of his, they killed my daughter, you hear me!"

"Martha, that's not true. I understand your feelings, because I too was filled with the same thoughts earlier. Today when I met him after the funeral, he told me a few things that startled me. I think you should know them before you declare him and his little baby as the killers of your daughter."

"No Jason, nothing in this world can make me hate him less now. He and his whims and fancies made my daughter take such a big risk. She risked her life for that man!"

As I said those words, fresh tears started streaming down my face. He wiped them slowly with the tip of his big wrinkled thumbs. He swallowed the lump that formed in his throat and said, "Just listen to me Martha. If you still think the same, I will never again talk about Edward in this house."

I took a deep breath and wiped my tears and nose with the apron that was still tied around me. "All right Jason. Tell me what that man has told you."

"We both know that Janice was always a kind and compassionate child. She was so happy when she told us about Edward, you remember that? When you were unimpressed by him, she was really worried. She had asked me to talk to you, to know what made you dislike him. The only reason you regarded him unsuitable for her was…"

"That he lived in another city."

"She knew you loved her so much that you didn't want her to shift even to another city though it was just a few miles away. Seeing her love for Edward and having made a complete personal check on Edward I decided in favour of him. We tried hard and finally convinced you for him." A sad smile broke out on his face as he recollected those events.

I listened quietly and felt the wound being split open again by making me go back to those beautiful times when she had gone berserk with her marriage arrangements. How beautiful she had looked that day! How she had cried while she walked down the aisle with her father! It had been the best and the worst day of our life. It was until yesterday.

"After she left, she always asked me about you. She was worried that you would be anxious about her. She and Edward tried in their own little ways to make you feel that Janice was just a phone call away; that your little girl was always around for us. For you. Then she had been informed of her pregnancy."

I remembered how happy I had been to learn about that. I was going to become a grandmother. I was as excited as Janice was. Our lives were filled with new energies and joys.

"That was the last thing she truly shared with us."

I was confused by these words of Jason, "What do you mean?"

"She even hid this from Edward. She didn't want anyone of us to know. It was her decision to have this baby in spite of the warning by her doctor. She hid all her reports from everyone. She would visit a different gynaecologist when she went with Edward while her case was being handled by another doctor. I never knew our Janice could be so secretive. She was so happy about this child that she forgot the impending doom that lay before her. That's what finally happened. As soon as she had the baby, her condition started deteriorating. That's when she told Edward about it. She thought it would be just a false alarm that her doctor was creating. She hadn't realized her folly until it was late."

"Edward was happy and proud yet he was shocked and broken at the same time. He didn't even know if he should celebrate the birth of the child or sit and grieve at his wife's decision. So he called us and we drove there. After that you know all that happened."

"How could she do this? Why did she do this?" These words came out of my mouth as I was filled with sorrow and anger.

"Edward says he never had asked for a baby. Rather he was glad it wasn't going to happen soon for he was trying to set up his business and felt they would have more time to themselves till the child comes in. Janice wouldn't listen. After her first miscarriage, she was heartbroken. Do you remember?"

"Yes. So the foolish girl let the baby survive at her own expense."

"Isn't that what a mother's heart is all about?" Jason remarked sadly.

I realized how I had been wrong. I had totally misunderstood my son-in-law. He wasn't to be blamed. Was Janice to be blamed? No. She too couldn't be blamed. She just wanted to have a child. She always had loved children. Her first miscarriage had instilled a fear in her that she would never be able to have her own. She had nearly gotten into depression. Edward had done so much to get her out of it. How did I forget all of that?

As thoughts started rising in my mind like a raging tempest, the flow of tears from my eyes wouldn't cease.

"I have been so wrong Jason," I said as I covered my face with my hands.

"You haven't been Martha. It was just the love of your daughter that had blinded you. I know even Edward would understand that. There is one thing that I had in my mind, which I want to discuss with you."

"What is it?" I asked trying to control the quivering in my voice.

"I was thinking of asking Edward to give Janice's baby to us. I want to see her grow with us. The little girl is the only thing we have that belongs to Janice. I don't know if Edward will agree but I want to try it. What do you say?"

I was dumbstruck. What could I say? "Are you even aware of what you are asking me Jason?" I shouted at him.

He tried to pacify me but it wasn't going to work on me. I stated in clear words that that girl had killed my daughter and I was not going to accept her any way in my life. She was a murderer. A child who killed its own mother cannot bring peace to her mother's parents. She would never be accepted as a grandchild by me and I would never forgive her. That was the last thing I said before I walked up to my room. We didn't speak after that, as Jason knew he was not equipped to make me change my decision and I was not in the state to understand his stand. My anger towards Edward had subsided but my hatred and pain hadn't. That child wasn't going to be allowed or even invited in my house, ever.

Days after that went in discussions and silence. Ewan, Matt and Jason felt that I was being too harsh on Edward and his baby. They all always liked him and now too they didn't see the pain their words had on me.

"Mom, you should see her. She is so much like Janice."

"Martha, you should really think about it seriously."

"Mom, that baby is the last thing we have which belongs to Janice. Let's bring her home."

In all this, questions loomed in my mind. Why was Edward ready to leave the child with us? Why didn't he want to keep his daughter for himself? Is this the love he had for my daughter? Was this why he had begged for her hand in marriage? It infuriated me more than anything that he was prepared to leave his first child away from him. I just needed answers and only one man could give those answers to me.

———

As I waited at the rocky area around the shore, my thoughts kept running in all directions. They were creating doubts and trying to look for the various reasons. When a person is afraid of facing something, he starts making excuses and his thoughts move hysterically, analysing all the possible solutions. Some of these can be so negative and disheartening that you start getting influenced. My thoughts and hatred were aimed at Edward here.

Just then I saw a girl walking towards me. She was a young girl, probably in her mid-twenties wearing grey top and black jeans. She closely resembled my Janice, probably it was the age or the way Janice would always prefer jeans on her visits to the beach. Her height and movement too were so similar to those of Janice that for an instant I felt it was Janice walking towards me. I wished and thought maybe all that had been happening around was nothing but a dream. Maybe my Janice was right there, walking towards me, smiling at me.

She had a small bag on her shoulder and slowly as she got closer I realized how foolish my thoughts had been. How deceptive my mind and heart were! She was nearly the same height and age; so were her blue eyes and the freely moving golden hair. Her radiant face, her thin naturally pink lips, everything was so similar to Janice's, yet she wasn't my Janice. Her straight nose and the dimple in her chin were features that set her apart from my daughter.

"Hello Ma'am!" she said as she stood beside me.

"Hello!" I only uttered that word and tried to avoid looking at her. We just sat there silently for a couple of minutes.

The close resemblance brought a tear to my eye and I wiped it off with the back of my hand.

"Sometimes, some things remind us of people who are so special that you wish they would come back breaking all the rules of nature."

I was amazed at her words and looked at her. She didn't look at me; her eyes were moving across the waves of the ocean. In a soft and melancholic tone, she said, "Life is unfair, isn't it! Life isn't unfair all the time. It is on us to take the things that life throws at us and realize the fairness in it. No one is burdened with pain more than what the soul can endure. Yet sometimes, due to that pain or suffering, we intend to lose out on the other side of it. To ease your pain, you have a blessing waiting to enter your home. You are so stuck with the woes that you are turning a blind eye to it. You are driving it away though it is knocking on your door."

Her words were making no sense to me. Pain – I knew what it was for me. Where was the blessing?

"You are seeing things just from your perspective. Think about the other one who too has lost someone. He might just end up losing the second one for your sake. Think about the one who will end up empty handed at the end of it all. Yet he will do it, because for him that someone's words hold more value than even his own suffering. Some promises are too difficult to be kept, they might just wreak havoc but you do not break them, especially when they are made.... on deathbeds."

As I tried to absorb all this she kept saying, nothing made sense to me. She turned towards me now and said, "Let him speak. Listen to him. Don't be judgemental. Just listen and then decide what you think is right."

After having said all that, she started walking away. I was shocked, this lady walks towards me, tells me things that make no sense and then she just walks away. I just saw her move a little and then my eyes fell on him.

"Hi Mom!" Edward's voice reached my ears as I sat watching the sea gulls fly about. The beach was the only place where I could spend some time alone. Jason and the boys wouldn't have let me speak to this man and ask him the questions that were running in my mind. I turned over and saw him standing at an arm's length from me. A fortnight after Janice had left this realm for another and you could see the effect on Edward.

He had lost a lot of weight and his chin was covered with stubble. He hadn't shaved since that dreadful day. His face had gone all pale and his eyes carried sadness in them. He smiled and it took a lot of power from within to give that unreal smile. I had been so uncaring that I hadn't even once glanced at this man. His broad shoulders now were drooping forward and his green eyes had lost the shine I had always seen in them. His forehead had recently formed lines while his lips were chapped. He was broken, just like me, just like Jason.

Probably he was as shattered as I was. In these fifteen days, he never tried to break the ice with me. He was in contact with Jason and my sons but not me. Instantly all the remorse and sadness I felt for him left me and I was ready to get my answers from him. He was alone just I had asked him to come. He didn't bring 'her' with him.

"Hello Edward," I replied back and crossed my arms across my chest. I sat like a stone there and wanted to keep myself like that while I spoke to him. I didn't want to break down before him. He didn't deserve that!

"You asked me to meet you here. Is everything all right, Mom?" he softly asked as he stood beside me.

"Edward, why didn't you tell us that this time it was a risk?"

He took a deep breath and replied, "I wasn't aware of it myself. Whenever we went to the gynaecologist, Janice would make her assure me that all was fine. The doctor would always say everything is under control. You know how Janice is…." His voice choked when he realized his mistake. He continued in a sad voice.

"She didn't let me come to know about anything. She was so secretive about it and I thought it was due to her first miscarriage that she was being so protective and keeping all things hushed. I went for all the ultrasounds, yet I was also kept in the dark like all of you. She didn't let me know because she knew I would never have gone ahead with this baby. I would have asked the doctors to care about nothing but Janice's life. If only she knew how much I needed her and loved her…."

He couldn't speak further and somewhere my heart softened for him.

"Yet, this child of yours, this girl whom my daughter brought into the world risking her own life, you are asking us to take her, why? Isn't she the last thing you have of Janice with you? Don't you want to keep her with you? Why do you want to give your child to us? Is it because you don't want to be reminded about Janice in future? Is it because she is too big a responsibility now that her mother doesn't exist? How is it that the father in you is unattached to his own child? Answer me Edward." Without stopping I aimed all the questions at him. I spoke with such firmness that my words stung my own ears, so I knew they were right on the spot for Edward.

He turned his face towards me. There was a confused look on his face and his eyes seemed to question me and my words. His eyes were filled with the salty water like that of the ocean. He raised his hand and placed his palm across his mouth. I saw him swallow down the pain my words had caused him. His eyes turned back to the waves of the ocean that lay ahead of us. He took a few deep breaths. I thought he would just leave my questions unanswered and walk away.

After five minutes, he finally broke the silence that had prevailed between us.

"It is not my decision Mom. I would never think of doing this. It is no more in my hands. I had promised her. If anyone else would have asked me to do this, I would have rejected it outright but this was a promise she took from me. A promise she took at her deathbed. Now I have no choice; though it hurts me more than anything. It was Janice who asked me to do this. She said that her Mom and Dad would not be able to bear this pain and suffering. She wanted me to give our daughter to you and Dad. You know what, at the end, if you step into my shoes, you'll realize that, I am the one who ends up losing everything in this."

The moment the truth was unveiled before me, the pain rose up higher in my chest. I didn't want to but my tears started pouring out on their own.

"Janice!" I whispered and Edward turned towards me. I put my head in my hands and started crying. Edward closed in the distance between us and placed his arm around my shoulder. He made me walk a few steps and seated me on the huge rock near us.

"Mom! Please Mom. I didn't want to tell you all this. I felt that if I hid this, I was not being fair on the promise I made to Janice. Every morning I would get up thinking what if you said yes, what if I had to give away my little baby. No one knows how much it pains me to do this. I will do it as it was Janice's wish. Her wish, this being her last wish, means a lot to me Mom. So I couldn't hide the facts from you. I have always loved Janice and will continue to do so always. My child is the only reason I have tried hard to keep myself composed. She is the little ray of hope that is keeping me alive. I am living for her and will do so till she needs me. It is you and Dad whom Janice has given the responsibility of her daughter."

We both sat there - companions in solitude and grief.

"Martha! Here you are!" I heard Jason join us.

"Hi Dad!" Edward exclaimed as he shook hands with Jason.

"What happened?" Jason asked me.

"I have made my decision Jason," I said as the tempest of thoughts in my mind had rested and the storm had died down.

Edward looked at us with a smile. Jason was amazed at the serenity I was sharing with my son-in-law. I held Edward's arm and holding Jason's hand I announced my decision.

"Janice's baby will stay with us."

Looking up at Jason's face, wiping the lone tear that fell from his eye I asked him, "Are you ready Grandpa dear, for sleepless nights ahead?"

The men around me had a soft smile spread on their face and I knew my little Janice was smiling too wherever she was.

Edward left soon. He offered to drop us home but I wanted to be alone with Jason for some time before we went home. As I linked my arm in his, a wonderful sight lay before us.

While the sun was going down, the sky was filled with shades of orange and blue and purple. I saw a train of white balloons rising from one corner of the beach. All the pink balloons reminded me of Janice's baby girl. I strained my eyes to see who was leaving those beautiful balloons into the sky. I saw a young girl, holding many more balloons in her hands. She was wearing a grey top paired with black jeans. Suddenly something struck my mind. I remembered someone telling about how a girl was out in the world... young...beautiful....and always had .... colourful balloons.

My life too had been touched by the girl, we all call......

The Balloon Girl.

A Father's Heart

Walking into the station, I bought a ticket to Holmsville. The train was to arrive in about a quarter of an hour. I had time to observe the hustle bustle of the town as the sun had just stepped into the horizon. Men and women, dressed in formal wear; rushing to reach their seats in the offices.

Observing people is something which amazes as well as annoys me. I get amazed to see an ocean of humans, moving from one corner of the city to another for the fuel of life. It is indeed amazing to see the amount of energy they expend to achieve their goals, their targets and to rise in their careers.

You wonder, what annoys me?

The greed, the desires and the self-centered nature of man leaves me dejected. The man of today's modern progressive world has his focus on himself only. He is insensitive to those around him. He doesn't see the sadness, the sorrow, the tears or the worrisome frown on the other person's face. Man has become a machine, a robot. He is a machine with flesh and blood; a mechanical being with a heart but no feelings.

A heart without feelings; as good as dead!

"Erica! You look so beautiful, my dear."

I heard him say. His eyes were glistening at corners with tears. Tears that seemed to have spilled over from the edges of the eyelids, as the eyes were unable to contain them. His deep brown eyes were always so kind and compassionate.

He moved closer and kissed me on my forehead. My heart fluttered in my body. At the same time, it was brimming with emotions for the first love of my life. He was the man who taught me everything about life. The man who made me feel love and taught me to be strong. He was the man who held me every time I fell and made me stand back on my feet. He patted on my back each time I stepped ahead in life or stumbled. He was the man who always stood as an impenetrable wall between sorrow and me.

With tears in my eyes, I raised my hand to touch his face. It had been a long time since I had been so close to him. Those wrinkles on his forehead and the lines near his eyes added a unique handsomeness to him. The dimple on his chin was distinct and seemed to go deeper when he smiled. The silky, grey hair shined like a silver halo covering his head. Age had just made him look more elegant.

As soon as my fingers made contact with his cold skin, he started vanishing. Like white smoke, he evaporated just right in front of my eyes. A sense of déjà vu filled me. He slipped away from us. Just like that day!

"Dad!" I shrieked and my eyes opened wide. I sat upright. It was not the same anymore. The place was different. There was no smoke, no evaporating fog. No Dad. Like earlier, he had visited her in dreams, today again.

As my eyes searched for him in the room, they fell upon the white dress across the bed. There lay my wedding gown. The white dress sparkling in the room as the sun rays sneaked silently through the window glass. Teary-eyed I fell back on the pillow of my bed. Nothing seemed to fill the void Dad left. Not a day passed since that dreadful event, without his memory. Life had never been the same anymore. Dad had been the lifeline of the house and with him went away many things and what they had with them were just memories of the times he had been with them.

Life was a blissful experience all along when he was around. Being the first child and the only daughter of the house, people thought I'd be like my mother. I proved everyone wrong, when instead of my mother I walked in the footsteps of my father. The two younger brothers I had, paid the compensation of being born five years after me, for they were never able to catch Dad's attention and all his love was showered on me.

Mom was their safe haven whenever they did something to me and Dad got mad at them. She always complained that he was spoiling me. She loved me for she was the mother. She couldn't be partial in her love, but Dad was. He was all one-sided towards me while both of them pined for his love and care. I tugged along with him when he went for grocery shopping. I was with him when he sat worried while Mom went in labour. I saw him hold those twin brothers of mine. I remember being filled with envy, but soon he kept them back in their cots and walked towards me, rustling the hair on my head with so much love. I knew what he was trying to tell me, that I will always be his first child and he'd love me the most.

As we grew up, I saw Dad worry when his job was in danger. I saw him stand strongly while Mom panicked around after he lost his job. I saw him sleeplessly walk around in the house at midnight. I saw him stare blankly at the sky bothered about the upbringing of three children and their needs. I saw him delivering boxes when he worked as a delivery man. I saw him at the gasoline pump, sweating it out in the blazing sun. I had seen him struggle and fight hard. I had seen him jubilant and happy. I saw the tears in his eyes and the fake smiles on his lips.

The serenity of my room and the memories of the times with Dad were broken by the loud ringing of my mobile phone. I stretched my arm and groped for it on the side table. Having found it, I raised myself and sat upright. The name that flashed on the screen brought a smile on my face. My lips moved into a smile, uncontrolled by any muscle. It was Patrick.

I swiped my finger across the screen to accept the call.

"Good morning beautiful," his voice echoed in my ears.

I wiped the tear that still hung on to the edges of my eyes.

"Good morning Patrick," I replied softly.

"Ready?"

"For what?" I asked wondering what Patrick had in mind and if I had forgotten something. He could do anything. Most of them were unexpected things.

"What? Don't tell me that you forgot!" he exclaimed in a voice showing unhappiness.

A naughty smile was surely embracing his face; I could feel it.

"C'mon Patrick," I giggled. He was a drama king.

He spoke in a serious tone, "Erica! Don't you dare change your mind now. You said you were ready. Ready to run away with me."

I was right. He was up to something. "Patrick … I can't." I had to play my part now in the drama he had started.

With a sad voice I continued, "You know I can never do such a thing. I can't run away like that."

"Don't say that. You know I hate it when you answer in the negative when it comes to being mine." In a jiffy that jovial mood changed into a serious one.

"I'm sorry. I didn't mean to upset you," I replied.

"Ready or not my love, I am coming in a few hours to take you away," his voice turned sultry as the words vibrated in my ears.

"I will see you then," I replied.

"Love you, sweetheart!"

"Love you too."

I heard the phone get disconnected.

As I lay back on the bed again, I reflected back on the time I had met Patrick. After Dad had gone things were never the same for me, for all of us. Since he had stepped into my life, the darkness that had engulfed me had started to recede.

We met at a bookstore. After Dad, books became my best friends. I became a quiet and serious person. We kept bumping into each other often. Soon those unplanned meetings turned into planned dates. Numbers were exchanged, likes and dislikes discussed. I found it easy to share my feelings and pain with him. Slowly the ship of friendship reached the shore of love.

A year of passed from friendship to courtship. Mom liked him too. Two months ago, things finally settled between us when Patrick proposed to me. His proposal was a beautiful thing to have happened to me. I knew our relationship was growing but I was still skeptical of taking the next step. I was apprehensive of taking such a vital decision without Dad and his guidance. All this was in my mind while Patrick had his own ways of winning my heart.

Our days were quite the same. We met, talked about books and ourselves, had a cup or two of coffee and then said goodbyes. Patrick was an assistant manager at the Pizza Hut franchisee, two blocks away from my house. I was working as a research associate for a private company. We got back to work if any was left and then chatted till the wee hours of the night till one of us fell asleep. This was a regular day for us. That day everything seemed the same yet it was all so different.

When we met on that eventful day, he was carrying a package. He said it was a copy of *A Walk to Remember* by Nicholas Spark that he had brought for me. I was eager to own the book of my favorite author. It was wrapped in bright red gift wrapper and a red rose was stuck across it. He didn't let me unwrap it there. Surprisingly he was in some hurry while we had our coffee. He quickly left saying it was something urgent. As he walked past the door of the cafe, he turned and said that he would be waiting to hear from me.

I stuffed it into my bag and started walking home. After dinner and a little chat with Mom I went into my room. As I lay on my bed, I remembered the book given by Patrick. I pulled it out of my bag and unwrapped it slowly. My joy grew when I saw that it was a hardcover edition.

I slowly caressed it with my fingers and I turned over the cover. What I saw left me speechless! There were no papers inside. No story to be read. There was a cardboard frame stuck inside those hardbound covers with a small part cut off. Embedded in that space, was a tiny brown box. Intrigued, I slowly pulled it out of the cardboard.

A gasp escaped my lips as a bright red ruby was sparkling in front of my eyes. It was a small tear drop shaped ruby surrounded with smaller white stones. All of them, fixed on a gold finger ring. A little heart shaped paper was attached to it like a tag. As I opened the heart I saw his words, in his own handwriting.

'You opened the heart of mine,
And passed your radiance, making it shine.
You know that my heart is filled,
with abundant love for you!
I have not much to give you,
Except for my companionship so that you're never lonely!
I just have one question for you; I wonder what the answer might be!
I'm waiting for your call, to tell me if you'll.... Marry Me?

I was expecting this to pop up sooner or later, for we were steadily moving ahead in life. As I was aware of the question, I was ready with the answer too. I had no other reply except a YES. That night we couldn't sleep and spoke till the early hours of the morning. Patrick formally spoke to Mom asking for my hand. That day I missed Dad the most. I wanted to know if he was happy of my choice. I wanted to know if he approved of him. He always said that Dad would never have liked him because my love would have got divided between the two of them. I smiled sadly but I wished he had been there and seen my happiness.

Patrick convinced Mom with his sweet ways and the D-day was fixed for 20th November. That was Dad's birthday. Finally, the day had come. It was today!

I stepped down the bed and pulled away the curtains. As the sun rays tiptoed into my room, they got reflected like glittering stars by the white wedding gown adorned with pearls and satin ribbons. Mom had designed it with so much love that each stitch and each thread was special for me.

As I moved my fingers across the smooth fabric of the white cloth, I was reminded of Dad. White colour always reminded of him. It was his favourite colour. His suits were mostly white. He loved his white crisp shirts. He loved white roses. He was not a memory for me. He was living in my heart. Dad would always live with me, till I breathed and my heart would beat.

The knock on the door brought chaos into my room as my friends and cousins barged in. the wedding day havoc began. Hours passed with everyone running here and there, looking for their pins, brooches, shoes, hair clips, flower crowns, tiaras, coats, ties and every tiny thing. It was noisy undoubtedly but it was wonderful to see everyone so happy and excited. The last picture taken of mom and the twin brothers with me was an emotional affair. We all knew whom we were missing.

As I sat in the car to drive to the church, it pricked my heart that I was to walk down the aisle without my Dad. Nathan, my brother would walk beside me. Tears brimmed up my eyes but I had to live with the fact that Dad wasn't there with me physically. He would always be in my heart and exist around spiritually but these things would happen without his presence.

I closed my eyes and wished. If only I could hug him. If only I could place my hand on his chest and feel his heartbeat like I used to. If only!

As I watched the lush green grass, the meadows and the hills passing by, it felt soothing. It had a calming effect on my heart and my soul. I knew I was doing the right thing. I just knew. My heart said so, or was it his heart!

"Sir, your stop is near." The young man who was seated beside me brought me back to the present, the reality I had to encounter. Again the thoughts swung like a pendulum, questioning me if I was right or wrong. Was it really a good idea to walk in? I was invited, yet was I expected?

As the train stopped, I bade farewell to the young man with the freckled face and stepped down. Everyone was walking along. Caught in their own turmoil and troubles, people just walked past. I wished there was someone with whom I could talk and share my questions. Someone who would tell me that it was absolutely right to do what I was going to do.

I walked in slow steps but someone was in a real hurry. A small push was enough to make an old man like me lose balance. As I stumbled and was going to fall face wards on the pavement, I felt a soft arm across my shoulder that stopped me from the fall.

It was a young woman in a light pink dress. She had a glowing face and sparkling eyes. She smiled as she pulled me up. I am an old yet strong man. She was able to make me stand on my feet and softly asked, "Are you all right, Sir?"

I nodded in the affirmative. She held my hand and made me walk to the bench near the signboard stating the name of the town 'HOLMSVILLE".

As I sat trying to breathe slowly, still reeling under the effect that the fall might have had on me. She brought me a bottle of water and twisted the cap.
"Please have some," she said.

I took the bottle and sipped the cool water slowly. The anxiety within me started ebbing and I started feeling better. As my eyes again fell on the signboard, I recollected the real reason I was here.

"Is everything fine?" the soft voice of the girl reached my ears as she placed her soft hand on my shoulder. She sat down beside me and waited for me to talk.

After a long breath and a few more sips, I was able to answer, "I am fine dear. Thanks for helping me. I still wonder how bad that fall would have been for the old bones and frail heart of mine. I am really grateful to you!"

"Oh.... that was nothing. I couldn't have let you fall like that. You are one strong man, with the wonderful heart that beats within you."

Something in the way she said 'wonderful heart' stirred me. Did she know me? Was she someone I wasn't able to recognize? Could she be the one? Was she here for me?

"Do I happen to know you, young lady?" I asked her hesitantly.

"Maybe. Maybe not." She smiled as she continued, "but I could know about you now. Probably I could help you. If only you'd want to tell."

As I had another sip of water and it passed through my throat, something in my heart whispered that she might just be the right person to share my dilemma.

I moved my hand towards the inside pocket of the white coat that I was wearing. I rarely wore white, but today somehow it caught my heart's fancy. I took out the little invitation card and gave it to her.
As she saw it, I knew what it had. I could tell it even without seeing it again. The cover had,
To,

Mr. Benson.

From,
Erica James.

Inside was a beautiful wedding card. The wedding of a girl named Erica with Patrick. Both were strangers for me, but the girl's name made my heart beat with a new found energy and emotions.

The wedding was today. The venue was The Holmsville Church, Holmsville.

When I received the invitation, I was sure I was never going to attend it. As days passed and the card kept coming again and again in my view, my decision started to waver and today in Holmsville I was. I was here to attend the marriage. I was going to the marriage of someone whom I didn't even know, but one whom my heart seemed to know so well. The only thing my wife could recollect about that name was it was the name of the daughter of **that** man. He was one special man in my life - that man and his family to whom I am indebted for the rest of my life. If I am alive and breathing, and the blood is gushing in my body, it is because of that noble man and his courageous and kind family.

"You are here to attend a marriage. That's amazing!" the girl exclaimed.

"I don't know if I should go there or not," I said in a sad tone.

"Of course you ought to," she said with conviction.

"But I don't know why she invited me. I don't know who the bride or the groom is. I just have an intuition that this Erica is the one I have heard about. Do you think it is right for me to go there?" I asked.

"Who is this Erica?" she asked innocently. That was enough for me to tell her everything.

"Two years ago, I was in the hospital. My heart was getting weaker and weaker and we were advised for a heart transplant. For weeks the medicos tried matching the ones they received through organ donation but none seemed to match my requirements. Until one day, when the doctors finally said I would hardly survive few more hours without a quick transplantation. I had lost all hope that day. I was just counting the minutes, waiting for death to darken the world for me."

"Suddenly there was an emergency case that was brought in the same hospital. The man was seriously injured. He was badly hit on the head. The man's family was worried and pleaded to the doctors to save his life. I was in the ICU too and was observing the happenings sadly. It was like seeing beforehand something that I was awaiting. Pain. Tears. Death."

"I prayed for the poor man and his family. A few moments later, a doctor walked into my room and asked for my case sheet. He walked out holding it. I wondered what they were going to do once my turn would come. Slowly I closed my eyes as my wife Anna held my hand, chanting her prayers. Death lets you know how helpless you are in the face of life and reality."

"'Are you sure doctor?' I heard Anna ask with hope evident in her voice. 'Yes,' boomed the male voice near me. I slowly opened my eyes and saw the doctor looking at me with a smile and a bright smile was on Anna's face as though someone had just injected some magic potion into her lips. 'What happened, Anna?' I asked. She was beaming with joy. I couldn't understand what could have happened in these few minutes that I had slept. 'We have a donor, Ben!' she said as her voice quivered with emotions."
"I was surprised. How did this thing happen! 'All the details have been checked and we find that this person's heart is all fine. We will be able to transplant it in Mr. Benson's body and with proper monitoring he should be as healthy as before.' The doctor

shared the details. Just then it struck me, 'It is that man who was brought after the accident, isn't it doctor?' He sadly nodded his head, 'Yes. We couldn't save him. Every passing minute he was losing it and went brain dead before we could even stop the bleeding. The head was hit badly and there was nothing we could do."

"The family was confused when we said that his heart was healthy and could be transplanted. The wife was hysterical but the daughter was strong enough to take the decision. Erica, I think that was her name. After a little discussion she was able to convince her grieving family. So they agreed to donate the heart to save Mr. Benson's life.' I was saved by a stranger and his family. The only thing that hurt me was that my life could be extended, only at the expense of someone else's."

As I ended the whole incident, tears clouded my eyes. When I turned to look at the girl, I saw her sitting with a strange serenity. She looked at me and asked, "You think it is the same Erica?"

"I don't know. My mind says it is foolishness to go. I am nobody for them. I don't even know why they sent this card. While my heart says I should go. It must be important for that girl, that Erica. She must have taken pains to locate my address and send it to me," I replied, still confused about what I was supposed to do. I was already there, so close to the venue, yet I was unsure whether I should attend the wedding or just go back home.

"Sometimes," she started saying as she opened her bag that was lying beside her and took out something, "we are incapable of stopping things that happen in our life. We are not even able to understand why a thing happens and what we are supposed to do. At such times, the mind and the heart are in a state of argument, a war. They cloud our thoughts and our feelings. There must be some reason for your heart asking you to go to the wedding. As far as I can understand, I feel it is the heart of the father which wants to attend his daughter's wedding, though it is beating within your body. I think you should go."

The moment she said 'you should go' the confusion in my mind vanished. My heartbeats that were hysterical a few seconds ago started to slow down, as though calmed down by her words. In that moment, all the hazy thoughts went away and I made my decision.

She handed me a bouquet of white roses and started blowing into a white balloon. Though a frail and delicate girl, she was quite comfortable as she blew air into those two little white balloons. She handed them to me and said, "Let's go."

I looked at her quizzically. "I am coming with you. C'mon let us go. I am sure you wouldn't want to miss seeing the bride walk down the aisle."

We both smiled as she helped me stand and we started walking out of the railway station. The confidence and firmness in her voice gave me the needed strength. Though a stranger, she was able to make me see what I had to do. She showed me the direction of the journey with her few words. Finally, I was sure of what I was doing here and that put all the doubts and questions of my mind to rest.

Moments passed after I reached the church.

'Erica, you look beautiful!'

'Erica, your wedding dress is amazing!'

The compliments kept pouring in and I had butterflies in my stomach. I didn't know marriage could make someone so nervous. The thought that it was Patrick waiting there, filled me with joy and hope.

As they announced my arrival to the guests, I started walking towards the church door. The ceremony was going to be outside the church, in the open space. It was all decorated in white and baby pink. My friends started lining up before me and the music started playing. Nathan walked towards me. I looked up at him. Dad's absence struck me again. A tear formed in my eyes and Nathan wiped it before it could trail down the cheeks. We both smiled and I tugged my hand at his elbow.

As I stepped out of the church, my eyes scanned the guests. Would he come? Will I be able to see him once? He was the only person who had something that belonged to Dad. Something of Dad that was still alive on this planet. Just then a taxi stopped. Maybe it was a guest who had arrived a bit late. The music played while I stepped out of the church. My eyes still were on that taxi. A young girl stepped down, probably in her mid-twenties. Maybe a friend of Patrick, I thought. She was helping someone get down. When the other person stepped out and turned his face, I stopped walking. Rather, everything around me stopped.

Suddenly the feeling of missing him left me and I could feel him there. Instantly I didn't feel lonely but blessed by the presence of the man who carried the tender heart of my father in his body. I hadn't seen the man's face earlier, but somehow I felt I had known him all along. In his eyes, I could see the warmth of Dad's eyes. In his face I could see Dad's reflection. Surprisingly, he too was wearing white. White - Dad's favourite colour. He steadied himself and stood there, holding white roses and little white balloons. It was just like Dad used to bring home whenever I was annoyed or sad. How could he have known this!

My arm slipped from Nathan's and I started walking towards the newly arrived guests. I didn't care what everyone was thinking as I walked towards the old man. The man and his companion briskly moved towards me. At an arm's distance, the man finally took my name, "Erica!"

The moment I heard the name from his lips, I felt Dad calling me out. I couldn't stop my tears. My hand flung to my face and tears rolled down. Soon I felt the old wrinkly hands of his wipe away my tears.

"Don't cry Erica. It's your wedding day. See, I brought your Dad with me."

As he said that, my hand reached out to hold his. He slowly raised it and placed it on his chest. I could feel the heart beating within him.

Dad's heart.

I could feel Dad's heart as it kept beating rhythmically, like I used to do earlier.

"Dad!" I said so softly as though calling out to him. I fell into his arms and cried. Those were tears of sadness and pain. Those were tears of happiness and love. The young girl helped me steady myself in that bridal attire. She placed my hand in his.

"Shall I be the bridesmaid, while we walk the bride down the aisle?" she asked me. I nodded with a broad smile and everyone started clapping loudly as I walked down the aisle with the man who had my Dad's heart.

When the marriage was solemnized, suddenly there were balloons that rose up in the sky. All white balloons. No one was sure where they came from. As my eyes hovered around, I saw that everyone was there, except for the young girl who had come along with Mr. Benson.

Was she the Balloon Girl?

THE END

Dear Readers,

I am not someone with magical powers or potions. The sole intention of my creation and existence is to make people think and wonder what if someone like me was around you when you needed some advice or clarity in thoughts. We all wish we had someone who would hold our hand when we are in trouble. The question is: 'Are we willing to be the helping hand for those around us?'

In today's world of advanced technology, of smart phones and trendy gadgets, of beautified selfies and social media craze, are we able to develop the basic traits of humanity within us? Do we update that feature of ours which the Creator has bestowed us with? Are we being humanistic in today's world of 'virtuality'?

When I walk into the streets and lanes, I find people who are either lost in their own successes or in their own pains and sorrows. Trust me, the others around you are in dilemmas of their own. They have their own pains and sorrows, their own troubles and hardships. If we all move around with frowns on our faces, is that going to help?

There must have been a time, when someone's smile made you wonder what joy is there in her life. It must have given you an impression that the person's life is all a bed of roses. Well, in most of the cases that isn't true. That person smiles because s/he wants to change the aura around him/her. The smile they carry is a gift for all around. They are blessed as they make attempts to brighten up the gloominess engulfing them.

Turn towards those beating hearts instead of those bright touch screens. Touch them with your kind words and smiles so that their pain is eased. The peace it will give you is incomparable. Smile often for you never know when it could make the other person feel better and add up to your pile of good deeds. Stretch out a helping hand when you feel that someone around you is stumbling. Be sensitive to those around you, for each one of us is responsible for peace within and around us.

Let the world see Balloons rising in the sky, left in the air by the humans, as each grief moves out of their lives.

With love,

The Balloon Girl

www.ingramcontent.com/pod-product-compliance
Lightning Source LLC
Chambersburg PA
CBHW020405130626
46549CB00006B/2441